Havoc Shore

Maureen Cullen

**Ringwood Publishing
Glasgow**

Copyright Maureen Cullen © 2025
All rights reserved

The moral right of the author has been asserted

Issued in 2025
by
Ringwood Publishing
Flat 0/1 314 Meadowside Quay Walk, Glasgow
G11 6AY

www.ringwoodpublishing.com
e-mail: mail@ringwoodpublishing.com

ISBN: 978-1-917011-11-2

British Library Cataloguing-in-Publication Data

A catalogue record for this book is available from the
British Library

Printed and bound in the UK
by Lonsdale Direct Solutions

For my late mother, Charlotte.

Contents

Introduction to Havoc Shore 1
The Cailleach of Redgauntlet Close 3
The Boy on the Bridge 11
Double Take 21
Tartan Legs 29
Kitten Heels 37
Havoc Shore 47
Fox Fur 53
Ring of Fire 61
The Midden 71
Trip Switch 79
Tiramisu 87
Isa's Pitch 95
Lang Craigs 105
Nae Bevvy 115
The Thin Place 129
Etcetera 137
Heron 141
It Would Take a Miracle 147
Next Stop 155
Blackbird 161
Passing Places 169
Awards, Prizes and Previous Publications 179
Acknowledgements 181
About the Author 182
Also by this Author 183

Introduction to Havoc Shore

This short story collection is about ordinary people in extraordinary situations, encountering the challenges in life many face, from poverty, unemployment, emigration, bereavement and discrimination, to abuse and family breakdown.

The stories are set from the 1960s through to present time, in the fictional town of Havoc which represents many communities on the Clyde, but is inspired by my hometown, Dumbarton. I became interested in the sixties after witnessing as a nine-year-old my grandparents' response to the Kennedy assassination. It was the first international event I was aware of.

I remember the shock and sorrow displayed at my grandparents' home who, like many Scots, had offspring settled in America. Maggie and Charlie, my grandparents, had cameos of the president and his wife, Jackie, on their living room wall and these fascinated me.

When I started writing short stories, this event came to mind and I set a few stories in that year. Kennedy retreated into the background of my own heritage as the characters grew and the fictional town of Havoc was born.

The short story form lends itself well to the examination of turning points in life, those moments or series of moments which shift our trajectory. They are a glimpse into a life, and they turn on an image, an idea or an event. They don't often resolve in the way novels do.

However, the joy of writing short stories, and reading them, is that each story is a complete entity to be savoured, even whilst they may resonate with other stories in a collection in terms of theme, character, place and language.

The stories in this collection are placed in largely chronological order and characters often pop up in other characters' stories as they do in real life, especially in small, tight-knit communities.

I hope these stories will strike a chord of recognition and resonate with readers long after they close the book.

1963

The Cailleach of Redgauntlet Close

Ross took a deep breath and flexed his quads before delivering the third kick. This time the lock broke, panels shattered, and the door swung against the lobby wall wi a solid bang. He gripped it as it flew back, halting it deid.

He still had time tae turn around, race upstairs tae his ain flat, lock the door, deny aw knowledge. Go eat his dinner, have a wee Glenmorangie, listen tae some Charlie Parker.

The smell and taste of disinfectant clogged his heid, ears, and throat. He hated that stink. It covered up filth, and it was filth he was aboot tae deal wi here.

How come it had tae be him that fixed this, when it was Annie's fault, standing beside him, egging him on?

He should've minded his ain business. Aye, tried that since moving in. But naw. One foot in the close and she was right in his face. 49 Havelock Road, four flats. He'd gazed up the winding stone staircase tae upstairs-left, the brass doorknob waiting tae be turned. It was aw writ doon on the rental agreement stuffed in his pocket. The flat across was empty. Privacy and peace. And he'd been impressed wi the building. The entry door tae the close was painted a postbox red, wi a hauf-moon pane above wi *Redgauntlet House* stencilled in frosted white.

Nice one.

Nae cracked paint, nae rusting banisters, nae damp running doon the walls. Original Victorian tiles on the landing floors and a smashing light fitting, a fuckin chandelier. Up a close. Jesus.

Up-market, in a nice part of town. Situated near the park and the train station.

Orderly.

He'd come tae appreciate order in his life and chanced a smile of relief, riffling through his inside pocket for the keys, but just as he was aboot tae take the stairs she appeared.

'Son, son … ur ye the new fella?'

Stumped.

'You, big yin. Och, look at ye. Whit height ur ye? Must be aw of six-feet-four. My, my, look at you …'

Trapped in the heidlights of her eyes, his heart sank. He wasnae here tae play guid neighbours or babysit auld women. A surge of weariness made him drop his canvas bag and grip the banister. He retrieved his hand, she might no like the sweary tattoo. 'Aye, that's me.'

She smiled, a full false-teeth smile that scrunched up her face, so she was aw fringe, glasses, and teeth.

Then she was off on one. 'Ah'm Annie. Mrs Nugent. Doonstairs-right flat. If ye need anything at aw, Son, jist knock ma door. Ah've been here forever. Moved in wi ma man, he's deid but. Died last year, heart attack it wis. Well, no exactly an attack, mare like when a clock stops. Done, finito. In his chair. Too fond of they fags, ye don't smoke dae ye?' The question was rhetorical, she hardly drew breath before she went on: 'Noo, ah'm here, aw day, every day, if ye need anything. Ah can take in a parcel, and don't ye worry aboot the close. Ah see tae aw that. And also …'

Would this spiel ever end? She stopped tae cough and he jumped in. 'Guid tae meet you, Mrs Nugent. Ah'm Ross.'

'Annie, call me Annie, ma mither's name … Don't let me haud ye back, ah'll jist show ye …'

Ross scarpered.

He'd been running the gauntlet ever since. The woman

viewed the building as an extension of hersel. Aye at the front door soon as he left the flat, or at the back door soon as he went doon tae the rear court wi the bin. How much dirty washing could one woman produce? The line was aye full of sheets and towels, or blanket after blanket pegged in a row billowing like sails in the northwest wind. Or she was sweeping the front path or mopping the tiles wi disinfectant. Must've been an industrial tank that delivered that. He'd even seen her at the bottom of the long yard, where the plot seeped intae woods, gathering sticks for the fire. Late at night when he went oot for his run, the snib unclicked. 'Och, it's yersel, Son. Jist checking.' The gummy face in the crack of the door was enough tae shrink yer baws.

She was a nosy auld hag awright, but every Sunday she left him a casserole or a pie at his front door. The first had a note. 'Ye need building up, Son. That big frame needs filling oot. Enjoy.' And he did enjoy they meals served in they new-style Pyrex white dishes wi wee flowers on. They tasted how they looked; no ower-salted, real chunks of beef, orange carrot, yellow turnip, proper squishy apples, tongue teasing cinnamon, layers of pastry that tasted of butter, and wee pearl totties wi green parsley smelling of the earth. Smelling of something long forgotten, something that teased his senses, that he'd known as a boy, before the shit hit.

He aye cleaned the plates, licking oot every morsel, handing the dishes back tae her when he went oot. Nae fear of missing her, she was aye there. He imagined her doonstairs, ear tae her front door, face contorted in rapt concentration, listening for his door tae squeak ajar.

She was there last month when the noise from the doonstairs-left flat drew him oot of his door. At first, he thought it was a party. Just some laughing and squealing, nothing sinister. The auld building was well insulated against noise, so this had tae be loud for him tae hear through the floor. He knew from his joinery courses that the space between the joists were filled wi ash and building debris. But the noise had accelerated tae the point he could pick up the odd insult. His heart shrivelled tae a stone as he recognised that tone of supercilious sarcasm, the blaming voice, the sourness. Then came wheedling tones from a female, a wail, banging of doors, greetin and pleas.

Violence from men tae men didnae fash him, he was strong and at one time had a reputation but hitting women wasnae on. Worse, it inflamed him, lit a fury he thought he'd tamed.

He'd loped doon the stairs two at a time catching Annie at her door wringing a dishcloth.

'Did ye hear that, Son?'

'Aye, is the lassie awright?'

'Bugger's back. She swore she wouldnae have him in the hoose. Efter the last time.'

Ross cracked his knuckles and stepped closer tae the opposite door. Aw was quiet. Och, he'd overreacted. The noise had set off his auld triggers. He lowered his voice. 'Jist a bit of argie-bargie, Annie. Away you go back in the hoose.'

'Ah'm fair worried, but.'

'How come?'

'Last time he put her in the hospital. Bust nose, broken rib. Och, her face. She looked like she'd been tore intae by a wild animal.' Annie's eyes filled up and tears ran intae the crevices of her skin. She took off her glasses and dabbed her eyes wi the cloth.

Ross leant doon and touched her shoulder, only tae pull away as if stung. He hadnae touched a woman in years. Retreating intae problem solving, he said, 'Phone the polis.'

She guffawed. 'He is the polis.'

Ross backed off shaking his heid, and made for the stairs. He couldnae lock his door fast enough. Trouble was he couldnae lock his door tight enough. Nor the door he kept firmly shut in his mind, the one that kept nausea at bay.

Running helped, running tae the point of breathlessness and pain, but the runs werenae enough for him. He'd join a sports club soon as he could. For now he lived in the moment. Present time was manageable, worrying aboot the future was pointless, and he had few memories he cherished. But that wee pat on Annie's shoulder kept at him. At the time he acted wi instinct, a natural act tae comfort another human being, but it unbolted other familiar locked-up intimacies.

Until tonight, there hadnae been any mare trouble from the doonstairs flat. He'd kept an eye oot for the lassie and met her once or twice in the close. She looked fine, nae injuries, bright and breezy even. A guid-looking woman, professional wi her skirt-suit, white blouse and briefcase. Annie was ower-egging it as usual, aye had a story tae tell, aye stirring her cauldron.

Ross forgot aboot that business and went oot tae work and his runs, passing the time-of-day wi Annie in the close or in the back court. She gave him delicious mince pies, and once she passed him a round of new baked, sugar-sprinkled, aw-butter shortbread. There was only one triangle left after the first go. Didnae matter, he was using up a lot of calories. Annie had laughed. 'Ye should be in a magazine, Son. Whit a physique. If ah wis twenty, naw, ah know, forty years younger …'

He kept up his running in the dark. That was beginning tae make no sense. People wouldnae remember the lad who used tae live here, who had returned tae make a life. The runs fuelled him, gave him energy, even at night-time. The feel of solid ground under his feet, the company of shadowy hills north of the Clyde valley, running wi the river on its way tae the sea, aw were familiar and comforting. As were the park, wi its bubbling fountain and beds jewelled wi summer flowers, where he used tae picnic wi his mother and grannie, and the avenues of trees, where in the autumn, he used tae fill his pockets wi the best chestnuts tae play conkers.

He'd started tae relax when he'd got caught again making his way upstairs. It was another one of those biting cold days when ye were full sure it would snow aw day, but it kept off tae dark fell and then flurried doon in the lamplight-like blossom. He'd put one white crusted boot on the first step when he heard a woman's cry. His heart stopped and he clenched his fists, but hearing the following run of *Jesus, Mary, and Joseph,* he realised it was Annie and that she'd maybe slipped and fell. He strode through the close and thrust open the back door tae find her lying on the concrete slabs, her hair bristling wi snow and her tongue bristling wi expletives.

'Och, Son, ah'm no hurt, except ma pride, but ah cannae get aff ma backside.' She held oot a quivering arm and after a moment's hesitation he leant doon, gripped her hand, swivelled his other arm around her middle and swung her tae her feet.

'My, oh my, ye don't know yer ain strength,' she said as she found her balance. 'Come away in wi me, tae ah get ma bearings.'

Ross was aboot tae protest, but a sharp look stilled that, and before he knew it, he was sitting in her lounge wi a mug of tea and a plate of scones on the side table at his elbow. The room was a frenzy of paraphernalia, every surface busy wi china plates, glass bottles, bowls crammed wi crystals, and on two side tables stood fringed lamps wi ivy leaves twisting their way up brass stems. The light from the fire shimmered and swirled on the walls, dancing ower framed photographs of Annie as an infant, as a small child, and as a girl, aw in black-and-white. There she was, as a young girl in her swimsuit, smiling intae the camera, standing on a sandy hillock, the Clyde's tide oot behind her. He looked closer, that was Havoc Shore tae the west of the town. And there she was, as a young and middle-aged woman in full colour. The moss tinted amber eyes, the fringe of hair, the personality blasting oot in forthright determination, aw instantly recognisable. The actual live Annie had tucked hersel intae the corner of an ootsize armchair at the fireplace, her eyebrows arched, eyes glowing wi spirited pleasure. Every time he took a bite of scone she nodded in approval and finally, as he wiped away crumbs, she said, 'Ah dae hanker efter a man wi an appetite.'

'Thanks again, Mrs Nugent, er, Annie. Ah'll be on my way up the stair.'

'No. It's early yet, and ah've a fine stew tae heat up.'

Ross squirmed; how was he tae get oot of this? Did he want tae get oot of this?

'Stay awhile, Son. Ah've placed ye noo. It's been hard, but something aboot yer eyes wis familiar. Stay tae ah tell ye how ah've remembered how yer grannie and me were great pals at the school …'

He'd stayed for his supper, stayed tae his belly was bustin, stayed tae the firelight in the grate had grown sleepy, stayed while she tellt him stories of his ain kin, stories he hadnae known hissel, and by the time he left he'd exposed his very soul.

Tonight, the noise had started up aboot nine o'clock. Ross had been watching John Wayne swagger intae a bar, the sound low, when he caught the build-up of voices. The same pattern of partying, weasel digs, banging aboot. He sat, heid in hands, unable tae quell the dread in his chest, unable tae stop the flood of images.

He couldnae stand it. He was up on his feet and seething. He threw open his front door and raced doonstairs.

Annie was pacing the close in her slippers, ready for bed in a pink quilted dressing gown, her hair in a net ower sponge curlers. Thank Christ her teeth were still in. 'It's too quiet in there. Whit tae dae? Ah phoned the polis, should be here by now. Go on in, Son. Break doon that door. It's locked, ah tried. Make sure she's awright. Wring that bastard's neck if ye huv tae.'

Wringing a bastard's neck was what had drove him tae where he was today. His insides flipped as he saw his mother, crumpled on the floor, blood pooling on the kitchen tiles, tributaries threading away under the table. She groaned as his stepfather stood ower her, ready tae throw another punch. Ross had roared, thrown himself at the bastard, grappled him, caught him in a neck hold and hadnae let go until he felt resistance fade.

Now, he shook the memories away and listened as he grasped the burst open door. Why had no one protested? The lobby of the flat was strangely quiet. Where was the lassie and her boyfriend? Annie was still gabbing, an urgent whispering, like the wind whistling in his ear.

'Wheesht, Annie.'

Something was ticking. The boiler maybe. Naw, it was the clock on the lobby wall. It was getting louder and louder wi every tick. Or maybe it was his ain heart. He felt sick. The sway of every ship he'd laboured on these past ten years was nothing tae the sway in his bowels and his belly now.

The whistling was insistent. 'It's awright Ross, ah know this is hard for ye, ah'm right here.' Annie's hand gripped his wrist like a swathe of knots. He looked doon at her lined face, her magnified, piercing eyes. Was aboot tae tell her tae go back intae her hoose and lock hersel away from him, from this. But he was held fast.

They took the threshold thegither.

1963

The Boy on the Bridge

I tried to slip into oblivion, but the late afternoon sun pouring through the arched windows stabbed at my eyes. Shimmying under the hospital blankets I pressed further into the mattress, my breasts hard and painful. I dragged myself up on one elbow and rolled onto my other hip, careful not to make the bed squeak. The row of beds struck me yet again as an incongruous sight in this old baronial drawing room with its ornate high ceiling, stucco centre rose, glass chandelier and painted cherubic figures decorating the walls.

As I settled, I caught Isa's eye. She rose on her pillows, one hand patting auburn curls, an inviting grin on her face; she was eager for one of her blethers. On the first day, I'd tried putting her off by studied concentration on a book but gave up under the force of her personality. Now, I managed a strained smile, knowing that she was only trying to cheer me. Encouraged, she threw her rolled up *People's Friend* at the lump that was Big Edna snoring in the next bed. Big Edna who proclaimed often and with authority, 'Hen, aw ah need's ma sequins and a soldier, and ah'm away.' This was Edna's way of lightening the gloom and once I had the measure of her, I appreciated it. It was hard to avoid such common parlance when billeted close together in a maternity ward.

This was my first experience of mixing with cleaners and factory girls. Although, these cleaners and factory girls were more welcoming than Rory's mother and her friends, who hadn't expected their pride and joy to return from London with an English girl on his arm.

That first time at the bungalow in Cardross, I'd extended my hand to his mother to be met with: 'And where exactly is South Cambridgeshire?'

Rory explained it was north of London.

'Oh, that far south,' she dribbled out, turning away.

Rory took my hand and whispered, 'Never mind, it'll take you fifty years, darling, with that plummy accent, to become a local.'

But I did mind.

So, I'd grown to welcome my companions' blethers because it relieved the tension, the worry that soon I'd be discharged home. Home meant having to face the future.

My waters had broken at the sink as I peeled potatoes for dinner. I hadn't quite got used to a house without help, but Rory was adamant we weren't snobs. I didn't much care for that perspective whilst peeling Ayrshires sitting on a low kitchen chair but better than standing at the sink with the front load and the back pain.

Dusk settled as Rory drove us to the hospital. It was that soft spring gloaming I liked, streetlights coming on, a purplish hue about the town and hanging over the Elvern. As we drove past Saint Aloysius' Church, the red granite of its walls the colour of old blood, I had a flash of our twins wrapped in the shawls his tetchy mother had been crocheting for weeks. And then another band of pain circled my midriff.

We reached Ardeer House as dark came down on the rhododendron bushes lining the driveway, their purple flowers hanging like bells, and I saw someone under a lamp on the bridge that spans the ravine linking the austere baronial mansion to the downhill path. The figure waved, but I paid scant attention as another contraction took hold and Rory hurried me through the hospital's high studded doors. Twin heraldic beasts greeted us as we passed.

Now, Isa sat beside me, and Edna across, feet dangling, dressing gowns gathered around our reducing bellies. Isa wore her daisy print slippers, my feet were folded in fine sheep's wool and Big Edna swayed her feet in high-heeled slippers with pink feathers. Rather like the Cinderella slippers in Woolworths' window that little girls could purchase for half a crown. Edna was more like an Ugly Sister than Cinderella, with her bleached beehive and puckered pockets under her eyes. But it didn't stop her from being a glamour puss. All she needed was that soldier.

We were quite alone in the ward. The hospital furnishings and bare floors didn't detract from the feeling of another time. A time of opulence and mystery. Opulence and mystery didn't impress my companions whose conversation usually turned around *they nothing but weans theirselves* nurses, the bairns, feeding, weights, that *bit o stuff* doctor.

Isa's baby was her seventh. All boys. 'I'm up for a football team,' she quipped, though the births weren't getting any easier. Big Edna was on her fifth and accepted Isa with great respect as the senior girl.

'Bump up, Lizzie.' Isa squeezed her rump in further. It was a bit too close, the rubbing of nylon at my hip, but she didn't notice that kind of thing, coming from a family of eight children, who'd all been squashed into a three-bedroom tenement flat, just off High Street. Isa's wiry hair was Kirby-gripped behind her ears and her Panstick line was clear to see on her chin where she hadn't rubbed it in enough. Her gold-specked, amber eyes reminded me of a vixen I'd once met crossing a wheat field in Cambridgeshire.

When I'd first woken up after the birth, pulses of pain wending through my lower parts, I'd cracked open my eyes to milky light and an auburn blur. A voice said, 'Want anything, sweetheart?'

I managed 'Water,' and soon a cold glass was at my lips. The dryness in my mouth abated with each sip but my cheeks were soaked with sweat.

'Have a guid greet,' Isa'd said with her lilting voice, and I realised I was crying. She perched on the edge of the bed, gripped my fist, her thumb-stroke firm and sure over my knuckles, and looked away, allowing me space, and something else, the comfort of another woman at my side.

My recollections were interrupted by a hard kick in the shin. 'Ye awright, Hen?' Edna peered at me, her black eyebrows squinting under the stiff blonde fringe.

Isa turned in my direction too.

'Yes, yes, I was thinking … well, never mind that … don't you think this place sometimes feels surreal?'

They both stared at me.

'I mean, it's different from the rest of the town.'

Edna nodded. 'Ah ken whit ye mean. It's no really like a hospital either and ah've been in a few. Even when the visitors come they dinnae stay long.'

'Aye,' Isa said, 'like my Angus, eh? He never stays any place for more than five minutes.' She shook her head. 'Ye aw know about this place, don't ye now?'

Edna laughed. 'Och, noo we're gonna get aw they auld wives' tales.'

Isa shifted up closer, the hem of her nightie rising over her freckled knee. 'That's as maybe no and as maybe aye.' She cleared her throat. 'My ain mother told me the story as her mother told it tae her. Now, I'm privileging you lassies here, for this is a story I'm supposed tae keep for my daughter's ears only. But given that even after seven weans she hasnae put in an appearance, I'm making an executive decision and christening you daughters of the McMenamin Clan for the day.'

Isa's voice calmed me, and I was a small child watching the words take shape in her mouth. We began a muted round of applause but stopped when she made the sign of the cross over our heads, which also put paid to Edna's giggles.

'This house here ...' Isa's eyes swept the room.

'This wan?' asked Edna, winking at me.

'Aye, this one ... This house here, wi its bridge and gully, is a special place.'

'Aye, it's a maternity hospital.' Edna raised her eyes to the ceiling.

Isa ignored her, merely raised her hand. 'A special place, like no other hereabouts. It's called ...' She paused and whispered, 'A Thin Place.'

'Looks wide enough tae me.' Edna kicked my shin again. I crossed my feet to stop them swinging.

'No thin as in no fat but thin as ... now how tae put it ...' She scrunched up her face in concentration. 'I know. Imagine ye're on the ice, skating.'

'Highly likely that.' Edna snorted.

'Stop it.' Isa slapped Edna on the wrist.

Edna pulled back her dimpled hand. 'Sorry.'

'Well, jist imagine a pond of ice. Thick wi ice except at one bit where the ice has melted and there's only a thin film left.'

'So ye'd fall in.'

'Ye've got it. You'd fall intae another realm.'

'You mean you'd fall over the bridge?' I interjected.

Last spring, Rory and I had strolled up Ardeer Hill, played hide-and-seek in the bluebell wood, picnicked at the pond called Spirits' Sigh, rolled up our trousers and tripped across stones and pebbles, water numbing our toes bone white. We kissed on the old bridge which scanned the narrow ravine next to Ardeer House. I wondered if it was safe, with its crumbling granite and low balustrade and Rory gave me a little push before hauling me back into his arms. We stood in one of the semi-circular parapets, listening for the tinkle of the stream fifty feet below but a breeze came up and we couldn't catch it.

'Well aye and no ... I mean it's a kind of doorway from

our world tae …' Isa looked around us, intent on the strongest possible effect, ' …the fairy world.'

Edna guffawed. 'Away, that's rubbish.'

Isa pursed her lips, nodded as though in prayer. 'There's proof.'

This silenced Edna. We leant forward as one.

'Dogs have jumped off the bridge, wi no reason at aw, quite happy their owners said … as if they were being led.'

'And whit happened tae them?'

'They fell intae the ravine and were killed.'

Edna snorted. 'That's hardly disappearing intae another realm. No very nice fairies, them.'

'No, some bad, some guid. But they've been seen.'

'Who saw them?' Edna was playing devil's advocate now.

'Oh, my gran when she was a wee girl. She had a full-blown blether wi a boy who jist walked off the bridge and disappeared.'

'Never!' Edna's eyes rolled.

'I swear it.' Isa made another sign of the cross.

I asked, 'Was he killed?'

'My gran ran frantic, tae this place, a private house then, and got the butler. They searched aw around, but nothing was found, and no one was missed.'

Edna said, 'Load of rubbish,' but she was fidgety and pulled her dressing gown tight over her chest as though bothered by a sudden chill.

I was sure the figure on the bridge the evening we'd arrived was a boy, a lad about twelve or thirteen, slim, very fair, his head silvered in the lamp light. I'd got out of the car and was waiting for Rory to lock up when a movement drew my eye. The boy waved to me but just then I bent over in pain and held onto Rory's forearms and, when I looked back, the figure had vanished. The hills, streams, and gullies of Ardeer Estate were a playground for local children, so I wasn't concerned, even if it had been rather late.

'Strange place to have a maternity hospital,' I said, 'when you think about it. Up here away from the town, this old place.'

Isa said, 'No it's the right place. Where bairns are born, where life begins, and …' She looked down at her slippers and then turned to me. 'And where bairns die. They need looking after. Some say the fairies come in the night and take the wee bairns that don't make it. Sometimes ye can hear them sing.'

A door banged in the bowels of the building. All three of us jumped.

'Best get ready for the bairns,' Edna said, shimmying off the bed.

Though I was relieved at the interruption, tears began to well up again.

For my boy.

They'd taken my babies away at once. The doctor came back into the delivery room, his face tight with regret, and I clutched at him. Rory was with him, his fists balled at his sides.

'Your wee girl is doing well but her brother, I'm sorry, we couldn't save him. Wrapped in the cord, not enough oxygen …'

They placed him in my arms, my perfect little boy. We named him George after Rory's father and later had him prayed over by the minister who assured us he was on his way to heaven. That seemed to settle Rory, but I didn't believe in heaven.

Isa was sitting on her bed staring full at me. 'Yer bairn'll be awright. He's being well looked after, don't ye worry. Your job's tae see tae the other wee mite. She needs her mammy and she's lost her other half.'

My daughter.

Somehow, I hadn't been able to call her that. Somehow

it was as if she wasn't part of me or that by feeding her, changing her and bathing her, I was denying my son. I was glad to see her gone when the nurses took her to the nursery. I didn't feel …well …I didn't feel anything for her. She brought on nausea.

Isa skimmed over, hip on my bed. 'I'm sorry, Lizzie, I shouldnae have said that.'

I tried a half smile. 'It's quite alright.'

'No, I don't think it is.'

'No.'

'I lost a bairn, you know.' She looked ahead.

'I'm terribly sorry.'

'Aye. In-between the third and the fifth.' She looked away to the window, the gold in her eyes sparkling.

I found myself taking her hand, a soft grip of pliable bone.

'Another boy, born dead, they said. We didnae get tae hold him. They wheeched him away. Said he was stillborn and no normal. Too big a head or something. It takes a while tae get ower it, but ye do.' Her half-crooked smile said differently, and I wanted to hug her, but instead I stared at our feet, her slippers, mine …

'Have ye gied her a name yet?' She coughed.

'No, actually I can't think of one. We had two to match you see, but now …'

'Try and come up wi something. It'll help ye see her better.'

Just then, the nurse brought my baby to me. I put one hand under her rump, one at her neck and held her at arm's length. She was so tiny, hardly the weight of a bag of Ayrshires. Gabrielle. That had been her name. I supposed it still was.

'Gabrielle,' I said, and drew her close.

Isa looked over her shoulder with the shakiest of smiles. She hesitated, then moved towards us, put her arm around us both, so close her ribs nudged my breast, and she kissed my cheek, her hand gentle at my nape. My daughter gave a little hiccup, which stabbed my heart.

The following Saturday, Isa and I left the hospital to lots of thumps and kicks from Edna who had another day to go. Isa went first, carrying her centre-forward new son. It was odd to see her dressed in a green cotton frock, pumps, pearl studded earrings and, of course, the Panstick line forming a mask on her face. Without thinking, I said, 'Hold up,' and took a handkerchief, spat on it and held her chin, rubbing the line away with firm strokes.

'Thanks, Lizzie,' she said, 'ye mind and drop in tae see me wi wee Gabrielle.'

Her address was safely zipped in my handbag.

It was a cool, clear day, and we left a few minutes after Isa. Rory fussed around us like an old granny. I passed Gabrielle to him and asked for a minute. He nodded and I strolled over to the bridge. I moved into the first semi-circular parapet, cautious of the low balustrade and the ease of tipping over.

It was a still morning and, far below, the stream tinkled like the voices of children. Pellets of sunshine dappled the foliage that lined the gully. Even though I didn't believe in myths and legends there was something eerie about this place. The air quivered with a viscous, rainbow sheen, a permeable film you could easily slip into. I leaned over, but an infant's cry startled me. I stepped away and hurried back to my husband, his arms full of our baby girl.

1963

Double Take

Winnie strikes up, takes a slow drag, slips into the reception area, gives her details to the sergeant on duty, and finds a spot on a bench. The place heaves with gloom. Townspeople haggard with worry stand in clusters. An officer calls, 'Winnifred Brogan,' and calls again before she realises it's her own name. He points to a set of double doors.

Smillie'd been polite enough with his request that day. After fawning over one of his clients, he'd cleared his throat. 'Mrs Brogan, er … Winnie, do you undertake any house cleaning work, in addition to office caretaking?'

Winnie had folded her duster in half, folded it again and then once more, achieving that neatness she liked. He rarely spoke to her directly; she was invisible in her overalls. That suited her; she had no time for this man with his slicked back hair and stained teeth.

She stepped back and to the side. 'Aye, from time to time. Just for a bit of pocket money. It'll have to be early mornings.' It had to be while the girls were at school, and Joe was at the Yards, so he'd be none the wiser about the extra cash coming in.

'Indeed.' Smillie swayed on the balls of his feet.

She put him out of his misery. 'I'll start on Monday, nine o'clock then, a trial you understand?'

'Very good of you.'

'It'll be ten shillings.' That was half again her usual rate.

'Perfectly reasonable. Thank you. It'll be some relief ... It's Hill Road, Glenorchy House.' He'd muttered on, backing away like she was the bloody Queen of England.

Winnie thumbs out her ciggie and follows the officer to a waiting room with rows of brass studded chairs. He leaves her alone and she lumbers to the middle, but feeling hemmed in, bum-slides over the chairs to the end of a row, her dress shimmying up past her knees. She yanks it down.

On that Monday, she'd dressed plain for work. She'd come off the bus at the municipal rose garden. It was splashed with reds, oranges and pinks and she'd smiled at the little cherub projecting water from his ding-a-ling. Her smile faded when she noticed two black-coated figures bustling towards her, brollies aloft against the wind. She didn't need to see their faces; it was The Crier and The Chronicle, two auld gossips she'd rather avoid or her new job would be common knowledge. Winnie sped towards the Bumbee stairs set into the brae and started climbing, careful of the crumbling stone flags, and turned into a tree-lined, well-heeled world. It was a grim morning, the rain coming at her in panels, but she was watertight in her rosebud Rainmate and flat patent boots. She read each name on the big gates until she finally reached Glenorchy House. Crunching up the drive, she was surprised to see Smillie's grey saloon parked in front of the garage. Winnie hadn't expected to see him. She thought his wife would be at home alone. He was always on to the clients about his good lady wife this and his good lady wife that.

The building was a dismal affair, cracks spidering across the front and grass spouting from the gutters. Giant rhododendron bushes, glowering without their flowers, dripped with rain. She pressed the nub of a brass buzzer and chimes rose far inside. The door creaked open and Smillie appeared in a diamond check dressing gown, feet poked into leather slippers, his spindly legs bare.

'I didn't expect to see you, Mister Smillie.' She glanced

past him into the gloom of the hallway.

The tramlines in his face deepened. 'Ah, Winnie, my dear, so ... grateful, er ... you could come.'

He didn't move to let her pass quite quickly enough, forcing her to breathe in as she skimmed by.

'Where's Mrs Smillie?' Winnie hung her coat on the stand.

'Regret she's gone to her mother's in Edinburgh.'

Other side of the country, wouldn't be back anytime soon.

His eyes twisted down and she caught the reek of whisky.

'Where's the scullery?' she asked.

He stared at her as though she'd asked for a hundred pounds and flapped his hand towards a door at the back of the hall. The eejit had nothing to say for himself, but she was ready if he tried any cheek.

It was a big room, dank and dirty with one poky window streaming with rain, the paint around the panes peeling. She made a beeline for the cupboard door where a mop's head leaned out dispiritedly. The wind keened outside, rain battered at the window, and water rushed down an eaves pipe, splashing onto the paving with a series of desolate splats. As the kitchen darkened, Winnie shivered and fumbled at a grimy switch. The room stuttered alight as she wiped her fingers on her pinny. It was like the rain was on her skin and in her bones, but this was work and ten bob was ten bob.

She filled the pail and shook in some Vim from the cupboard under the sink. The floor was covered in filthy rubber tiles, the sink was rimmed with yellow grease and the dirty pots on the cooker would have to be scrubbed hard.

Sniffing with distaste, she continued with her chores, quite forgetting about Smillie, until bent over the sink, her ears filled with the rush of tap water, she felt the weight of a hand on the rise of her bottom. The smell of whisky choked her; his breath was at her ear. She drove her elbow into his ribs. He groaned and, as she turned to face him, fell backwards onto the table, scattering chairs.

Winnie inched away from the sink. His eyes were full of accusation as he pulled himself to his knees. She knew that look and where it could end. It was Joe in his cups.

Her arm swung wildly behind her; her fingers clutched at a handle. The drawer stuck in its runners; she jerked it further. It came away, scattering metal to the floor. Too far to reach. Her body tightened, the last ladle settled, the vibrations ceased, the air filled with the sound of the old clock in the hall: tick, tick, tick ... Smillie was on his feet, groping towards her, his fingers trembling, white spindly thighs visible as his dressing gown slanted open. She skidded to the right and caught hold of a heavy pot. Its edge dunked skull; he grunted once and slumped to one knee, eyes bulging.

She ran, the drone of his choked laughter following her all the way to the front door, down the hill, and past the rose garden with its little cherub spilling water from his ding-a-ling.

In the waiting room, Winnie stares at the pattern on the tiles. Creamy, veined with orange, like real marble. She rubs it with her heel. Hard, no joins. Must be marble. Feels like it, looks like it, but looks can be deceiving. Actions can be deceiving too. And now she's here to explain her own. How's she going to do that? Except to say she might have been mistaken. How she wished she'd taken a moment to listen to the man. When she replays that morning, she can't be sure of events.

Maybe he'd touched her at just the wrong moment as she bent down and she'd overreacted. Maybe the look in his eyes was desperation, not anger. Maybe he'd trousers on under the dressing gown.

Maybe she should've taken that one beat of the heart to consider things. She could've turned and said, 'Can I help you, Mr Smillie?'

In one beat, life would've gone on as before. In one beat, she wouldn't be sitting in this waiting room. In one beat, Mr Smillie wouldn't be lying on a mortuary slab.

She could've sat him down on a chair at the table and filled the kettle. 'A wee cup of tea, Mr Smillie?'

The waiting room dissolves around her and she's back in that dreary kitchen, taking out two odd cups, one with rosebuds and the other yellow with a gold rim, and some sugar. The sugar has brown splotches and is hardened like cement, so she has to dig in the spoon to break it up. She finds a pot, a tea caddy and another spoon. There's a bottle of cold milk on the drainer. It must have been outside for a while; a bird's beak has punctured the foil.

The man sits with his head in his hands. Hands that are gnarled, hands without a wedding band. No woman has been in this kitchen for at least a year.

She pours the scalding tea. Adds sugar and milk to his without enquiry. Has her own without the milk. Sits a decent way off but close enough to hear him. He looks up. Winnie's forced by proximity to meet his eyes. He seems a man demented. Despite the smell of whisky, he's sober. She knows enough about drinking men to know that, but still his fingers shake when lifting the teacup so that liquid spills onto the table. She leaves it, even though it grates to ignore such a mess.

He raises the cup to his mouth and slurps. The noise aggravates her. The tea seems to give him back some control. His hand's steadier when he puts down the cup. 'Sorry, I've made a mess …'

'Not at all. It's your own house.'

'Forgive me … a mess … I forgot you were coming this morning.'

Winnie nods, takes a sip of tea, glad of its warmth.

He falls silent again, staring at the floor, his breath catching from time to time. Winnie waits. She's patient, not her usual busy self. The leak outside the window grows louder as if to invade the room. Smillie doesn't notice, he's encased in misery, chin at his chest.

She could go or she could stay. She could call a doctor. But if she did, what would she say? Mr Smillie's not himself, he's had a good drink last night, the wife's gone, the place is a mess, and he's in a right odd mood. Hardly an emergency. Bugger it, she'd have to sort this out herself. She does, with the skill of a psychiatrist. She listens to his story. The man has money troubles and is in over his head in certain 'business transactions'. His wife has filed for divorce.

Only one beat of the heart, and she wouldn't be sitting in Havoc police station, the tick of the waiting room clock forcing her back to real time. It ticks louder and louder as she listens. Her jacket's too heavy, making her sweat. She wriggles out of it, settles it on the next seat and smooths it flat. She looks down at her fingers. No rings. It's strange how one bad decision can make you face up to your other choices. If she'd known what Joe was like underneath, she'd have run a mile, but she'd been far too young to see him for what he was. A man with a mean streak the length of a washing line.

In the end, men were just not worth the unwrapping.

In the end, she could only swear to what she remembered.

The waiting room tilts as footsteps in the hall tap towards the double doors. It's time. She holds her breath, stares at the door ...

The double doors squeak. She gets up, her dress sticking to the warm seat. She pulls the fabric smooth.

'The Inspector will see you now. You all right, Ma'am?' He has warm blue eyes and a face crisscrossed with age.

'Just a bit nervous.'

Although she never saw James Smillie dead, every night she wakes up with the image of his dangling body, head at an angle, the silk dressing gown swinging gently as the rain drums on the garage roof.

'Come, my dear.' The officer holds her gaze. 'You'll be alright. Everyone who waits here feels the same way. It'll all be over soon.'

1963

Tartan Legs

Theresa had another go at the words she'd been practising. Practising was one thing. Saying them out loud to her mother was quite another. Maybe she should let the gale whisk her off the cliff into the Clyde at Havoc Shore, roll her down the Firth into the Irish Sea, and from there toss her like a cork, out to the Atlantic.

If only.

She'd just take a wee walk around the scheme to settle her stomach. Why her mother chose to live up here, the most exposed area of Havoc, high above the Clyde, she couldn't fathom. It was a right trek, so it was. As she turned the corner she set her brolly against the wind like a bin lid, but still a lash sopped her nylons.

She almost tumbled over The Crier and The Chronicle. One was the mother of the other, but they were identical. The hitch of the brolly, the spindly legs poking out, made them look like crows. Crows that might swoop on her head and peck out her eyes. Aye, like those in the Hitchcock film at the Odeon last week. She rubbed her stomach with the heel of her hand.

'Theresa, Hen,' they clacked, their brolly spokes jabbing her into the neighbour's hedge. Cold water seeped in from Theresa's neck to knickers. One said, 'Off tae see yer ma then?'

'Aye, aye, ah am …'

They leaned in, beady eyes bright. The other said, 'Maggie's lucky tae have a daughter like you. Round every Saturday. Why, jist the other day she said how she didnae know whit she'd dae withoot you and that braw man o yours. Poor widow wuman that she is.'

Theresa's stomach tightened again.

'Ye awright, Hen?' they both cawed, in unison.

'Aye, ah'm fine. Jist droukit.'

'Oh, ye can say that again. A body could get blown off the cliff ... and jist away tae get a pan loaf.'

A gust of wind rose up and wheeched them round the bend, black raincoats ballooning behind them as if in flight.

The latch of the gate squeaked as usual. Charlie said he intended to oil it after Mass on Sunday. Her mother drew a line at gardening, said that was man's work.

Mum's head floated in the window. Theresa fluttered her fingers. Thank God, it wasn't the weather for the Saturday trip to the cemetery, tramping down there to tend Dad's grave, Mum polishing the lettering, *James* and *Baby Liam*, her auburn head powdered grey, Theresa on the gravel praying.

Praying she'd hurry it up.

Praying for wings so she could stretch away, leave all the soil and supplication behind.

At the doorstep she collapsed the brolly, spewing ice-cold water over her shoes. The front door gave way as she turned the knob, even though Charlie had told Mum time and again to keep it locked. 'Maggie, yer a woman on yer ain and there's a lot of drunks and ne'er-dae-wells around here.'

'Ah'm no feart of drunks. Ah'll lock it when the dark comes down and unlock it at first light, as ah've aye done.'

The fight rose in Theresa's chest and flushed her face.

Everything was always the same: skirting boards dusted on Mondays, brasses on a Thursday, floors hoovered daily, coins counted out in columns for the milk boy, the paper boy, the insurance man, the coal man. Her mother ticked her life away to household duty.

Well, Theresa wouldn't be chain-ganged into drudgery.

She stepped into the lobby, soon breathing in a mixture of bleach and polish that set off a bout of sneezes.

Her mother stood at the kitchen door. 'Ye're no comin doon wi somethin, Hen? Here, gie me that coat. Go on in, sit at the fire.'

Theresa was helpless to stop the tickle in her tubes. Her coat was dragged off, nearly tipping her on her bum. She slipped off her shoes and they fair flew up into her mother's grip, landing at the fire in the living room. Sputtering into her hanky she followed them in.

Mum spun past like a wraith, and in no time the kitchen hatch pinged open. 'Ye'll get yer death of cold in that wee slip of a coat.'

No point telling her that the rain had just been a wee smirr when she'd left the flat and it was only up here that the gale blew. Anyway, her mother had already turned to the jigging kettle.

Theresa stood by the grate, shivering despite the spit of flames. Her blouse was pasted to her back. She plucked it out of her skirt, and leaned closer to the fire, scorching her legs just the right side of pain.

Mum came in with the tray. 'Ah made it nice and strong. Och, sit down, Hen, ye'll get tartan legs.'

When her mother bent to pour the tar, Theresa glanced up at the photo frames either end of the mantelpiece. Lovely Liam ... just a wee baby. Even after all these years she sometimes caught the scent of baby powder when she was in this house. Although she'd only been a toddler herself and could have no real memory of her wee brother, other than the small white coffin laden with yellow roses, her throat caught. Her mother's grief had taken root in all their hearts.

Liam's photo wasn't there.

In its place was her own wedding photograph. That was usually on the sideboard. She twisted around. No, in its place was some animal ornament or other.

At least Dad was still on the mantel. It would be easier if he were here. She would never have been able to marry Charlie if it hadn't been for Dad.

He'd said it first. 'Theresa has some great news, don't you darlin?'

She'd nodded with one eye on the door.

Mum's eyes had darted from him to Theresa.

He said, 'She's winchin Charlie Reid's boy. A nice fella he is too.'

Mum's eyelids batted. 'A ... Protestant?'

Her mother hadn't spoken to her for a whole week. Just took on a martyr's slump. Only fully came round when they got engaged and Charlie promised to marry Theresa in The Chapel.

Theresa twitched as her mother thrust the cup and saucer under her nose, spilling the scalding tea over her hand.

Mum fussed. 'Oh, my God. Ah'm sorry. Ah don't know whit's the matter wi me the day.' She rushed out, soon returning with a dripping cloth.

Theresa let her dab and wipe. The hand wasn't sore, but her eyes stung. If only Dad was still here, on his flock-worn chair by the fire, roll-up tight between his fingers.

On the eve of her wedding, he'd smiled his half-cocked grin, took a drag, rolled the smoke around his mouth, let it coil out. 'Aye, when ah wis a young man, masel, ah hid dreams.'

'Ye can still have dreams, Dad.'

'Aye, aye, but chances don't come round that often. Yer ma didnae like the idea of being a Ten Pound Pom. Naw, she wouldnae leave her ain mother.'

'But Dad, you should have made her go.'

Mum was still dabbing. Theresa concentrated on the

lampshade above her mother's head. When the letter had arrived from Australia House three weeks ago, Theresa had placed it on top of her whites in the dresser drawer.

Mum wittered on. 'Ye awright, Hen? Whit a carry on. Yer big brother's got a new job. In Glesga. He'll get the train, but. They'll no be movin anyplace. Ah widnae get tae see the weans as much. Mind that's no a bad thing. Ah've got ma ain life tae. Change is guid, dependin ...' She placed the teacup back in Theresa's hand before sitting down across from Dad's chair. 'Ah draw a line at pigeon! Imagine eatin pigeons. Dirty creatures. Rats wi wings. At the dinner he went tae. Funny stuff folk eat in far off places. Course, ah bet there's some lovely fruit ye can get abroad. Theresa are ye listenin tae me, Hen?'

Just as Theresa opened her mouth, her mother was away again. 'Ah nearly forgot tae tell ye. Hannah Gillespie? She's got cancer.' She spelt the word out as if it would blister her lips. 'Life's short so it is. If the fags don't get ye, the weather will. Don't get me wrong, there's a lot tae be said for the outdoor life ...'

Theresa tried a sip of the bitter tea. There was something different about her mum today. She looked younger.

'Ah want tae see ma weans get on Theresa, ye know that, don't ye?'

'Mum?'

'Aye?' She peered into Theresa's face, expectancy in her eyes. Mum thought she was pregnant. That was it. But her mother went on. 'Ah'm sure ye're goin under wi somethin. Ye look awfy ... peely-wally. It's the damp in this place. Ye aye had a bad chest. When ye were wee ...'

Theresa's insides seesawed. Mum counting the shillings for the bills, Mum stewing the tea in the pot, Mum tending the grave.

Theresa said it. 'We're emigrating to Australia. We've been passed and we're off tae Canberra in May.'

Mum's mouth opened and closed in slow motion. Theresa focused on the lips, the filling eyes, the lipstick and violet eye shadow. Lipstick and eye shadow? A lone tear sprang from the corner of one eye and a black thread trailed down one cheek. Mascara? She looked closer. Her mum had Panstick on, she hadn't rubbed it in right, but it was still nice. And rouge. Two dots on her cheeks. And her hair had been French combed into a flurry of bright auburn. Theresa shook away the haze. Mum was half smiling. She was quite pretty when she smiled.

Inching her cup and saucer down, Theresa tuned in.

'Och, Hen. Ah wis wonderin when ye were gonnae tell me. Ah wis under pain of excommunication if ah breathed a word of it tae ye. Father Mills heard it from Jack's mother-in-law's cousin who's off Charlie's pal's family, whitshisname? Remember her, she cleans the chapel house? Father thought ah should know but ah wis tae wait till ye tellt me yersel.'

'What?'

Her mother pressed her lips together, moved over to the couch and clamped Theresa's hand under her own. 'Och, ye cannae keep a secret in this toon. Don't get me wrong, ah wis heartbroken, ah am. At first ah wis going round tae yer place tae gie ye a guid talkin tae. Tae tell ye that ye couldnae go. But Father took me aside after the parish jumble sale. He looked me in the eye and said, "Margaret, you're thinking only of yourself. Your daughter must follow her own path." Yer a clever girl and ye'll never get on here.' She turned, smiled at Dad's photo and whispered, 'He'd never forgive me if ah stopped ye.'

Theresa closed her eyes against the nip of salty tears. Her mother's hand now stroked her hair, the other on her cheek, fingers soft as eiderdown. What? Theresa peeked through wet lashes.

'Mum, ye've had yer hair done.'

'Aye, dae ye like it?' She patted her lacquered head. 'Ah

thought it wis time ah bucked masel up.'

'What?' The fire had swallowed all the air in the room.

'Ye've got tae live yer ain life. Ah've got the grandweans and ah'll get the phone in. It'll be awright. We've come through worse and we're still in one piece.'

The dam Theresa had battened down burst. All the certainty in her life was floating away to be replaced with what? Joeys and sunshine? Joeys? Her head rubber-banded to the sideboard. A figure of a kangaroo with her joey peeking out of the sack greeted her, *Love from Australia* etched on its hat, a hat with corks hanging in a circle.

1962

Kitten Heels

I'd already said yes to the invitation, but Mum was a hissing serpent, and the negotiation could end in a sting.

'Mum, Amy Roberts is having a birthday party. Can I go?'

She was busy wi the wringer and the kitchen belched steam, but at least her hands were fully occupied. 'When is it?'

'On Friday …'

'No.'

'But Mum …'

'Nae buts, Kathleen.'

I didnae often resort to wheedling but I stuck my heid inches under her roseate cheeks, taking a blast of heat on my neck from one of Martin's nappies.

'Mum, I can still do the job, come home and go back to the party. Please.'

She sighed, dropped the nappy back into the tub, and put down the tongs. 'Whit time is it at?'

'Five o'clock till eight o'clock.'

She winced. 'Amy Roberts eh?'

'I can still go. I'll leave the party at quarter to six, dash down the road, pick up the packet and run back here. Then sprint ower to Amy's again. No one will notice a thing.' Morag was only nine and Rosie four, so it was down to me. Mum wouldnae do it, she'd the baby to nurse, and she was far too affronted to ask her pals. I sensed possible leverage. I could work this and use some of the credit I'd run up.

Her eyes narrowed and for a moment refusal set on her lips, then her face relaxed, her shoulders drooped, and I knew I had her. Maybe it was the eagerness in my face, or some memory of fun times past (though that was unlikely, this was my mum), or maybe she was just worn out. I pretended to be anxious wi anticipation, to give her the satisfaction of the indulgence. It wasnae often she had any of that. Finally, she said, 'Awright. Mind ye've got tae be there on the dot or else …'

I knew the critical nature of my task and the consequences of failure. There could be no 'or else'. I was living two lives, one responsible parent-in-lieu and the other would-be party girl in nylon sheath, kitten heels, and flick-out hair. Those kitten heels sure took some getting, and I wasnae about to sprint in them, so I'd have my sannies in my pockets ready for the dash.

On the day, aw my lies were suitably concocted to avoid failure. The excuse had to have the appearance of immediacy. I couldnae be called away. For a start there wasnae a phone in my house, we used the one in the corner shop. Nor could I ask anyone to rush up to the door and fetch me off on some emergency as this was only between Mum and me. I ransacked my brain and the obvious scenario fell into place. It was perfect.

Amy's house was in a private road, where people lived who had money and knew nothing of scrimping and saving for shoes or relying on the Provident for your school uniform or the Saint Vincent de Paul for a pram for your wee brother. As I approached the building, I fiddled in my inside duffle pocket to double-check I had my Snow White watch. The other pockets were tight wi my sannies and I couldnae actually display this relic from a younger Christmas.

I strolled up the crazy-paved driveway, jagging myself on

a stick of purple heather protruding into the path. The house looked smart enough, a semi-detached Victorian building, aw windows, blackened brick and brass knockers, one of those types my mum cleaned when she got the chance. She complained that the dirt in those houses was a mortal sin.

I bit off one glove and knocked the green door three times. There was no answer, though people milled around in the big bay-windowed lounge. Brightly dressed, teenage girls were giving it laldy to Elvis Presley under an actual crystal chandelier. I patted down my yellow straight up-and-down, pan-collared number. I was a skelf, probably looked like a colouring pencil, and to add to my misery, elastic bands held up my knee socks making my legs itchy so I had to lean down and massage the angry red circles.

After a few minutes shivering, I realised the outer doors led into an inner wee sanctuary, where you were supposed to ring a bell. I rang and rang and just as I was about to leave, Amy herself appeared in the hallway and opened the door. She was bright in a red velvet dress, but this didnae help her startled eyes and pale twitchy face. Normally she was dressed in school uniform like me. We both stood staring at each other in a kind of trance.

Gathering my wits, I strolled past her, head held high, remembering what Mum had said when she'd taken a precious minute out of her chores to lecture me.

'The Roberts think they're posh, but dinnae think anything of it. Ginty Roberts was Ginty McLeish before him and he's an odd bod. English Catholic, no the same as us. Rod up his arse.'

In the lounge, I was greeted by a bunch of girls from my school but the rest were strangers, most likely from the private school up the hill, neighbours of Amy's. I joined in the dancing for a while, gyrating to *The Loco-Motion*. It was aw a bit loud and Amy was absent, so I smiled my way through the throng and found her on a stool in the kitchen.

'Where's your Mum?'

I expected to find Mrs Roberts in the kitchen, but there was no sign of her. The noise in the lounge was growing louder and two of the girls were dancing on the coffee table. I'd never been to anything unsupervised unless you counted babysitting the wee ones. My mum would have a fit if she found out. More high-jinks and squealing came from the lounge and girls started to spill into the hall and kitchen, one shamefaced wi a broken ornament in hand. I took it from her and laid the pieces on the counter. Amy's eyes twitched like she had tics and she kept rubbing her hands thegither, bending back her fingers as if they were rubber, aw red-white blotchy as though blood pooled underneath.

My own house was a stress-pit most of the time, though in recent weeks a sort of solace had crept in, but I recognised trouble when I saw it. Sure enough, Amy burst into tears. I took her by the arm and shut the rest of them out, closing the door wi my heel and stared at her.

She blurted out, 'Oh Kathleen, my dad will be home soon and …' She drew a hanky from up her sleeve and blew into it hard. Balloons were being burst now to squeals of laughter.

Mr Roberts would be scandalised, he was in the Knights of Saint Columba.

I repeated, 'Where's your mum?'

Amy's face scrunched into ridges and folds where tears puddled. She pointed to the ceiling.

'Righto, I'll get her.' I took the stairs, two at a time.

'Mrs Roberts,' I called out into the upstairs hall. 'Mrs Roberts, Amy needs you down the stairs.'

At the end of the hall a grandfather clock chimed the half hour, its gold hand quivering ower the Roman numerals. I'd need to get out of here in ten minutes, tops. There was a toilet ahead, the sheen of white porcelain winking in the semi-dark. Amy's bedroom door was open, her uniform discarded on the floor, a teddy bear wi a tartan bow helpless on its back on the pink coverlet. A few hardback books were scattered at the side of the bed. The ceiling light was on and I pushed the door open a tad more, just out of nosiness. Gawd, this was a fine room, not like mine at home wi the beds close together and cupboards busting wi stuff. My books had to be kept well under the bed for fear of damage and an unaffordable fine at the library. A bump to the right jolted me out of jealousy. I turned and stepped down the hall, recognising a strong peaty smell that caused me to pinch my nose. I stopped at another door, this one only open a fraction, soft light spilling through the gap, wishing I'd never come to this blasted party. And what had possessed me to come upstairs? Something must've been up if this woman couldnae hear the racket. Maybe she'd taken ill. I knocked the door. 'Mrs Roberts?' I pushed the door open.

A Johnnie Walker bottle, without its plug, balanced on the lip of a large ashtray on the bedside table, three or four inches winking like honey. One black high-heeled shoe lay on its side on the Oriental rug and the other pointed toe-up to the ceiling on the nylon foot of the figure on the bed.

Mrs Robert's lilac party skirt had slipped down in abandon, hip bones nudging the material either side like wee rounded pebbles. Her white silk blouse had loosened from the waistline and slipped up to rumple ower her bra. A line of blonde down ran from breastbone to belly button ower flushed milk skin. One hand was flung ower her heid and blonde curls rioted around a doe-soft face. Her daughter's features were there, but without the mousiness. The other hand drooped ower a crystal glass upended on the floor, which had dripped a wet stain on the rug. Women didnae get drunk in our social set. My mother liked an Advocaat at Christmas and I'd seen the aunties wi a Babycham. I stood there far too long for decency, the sight oddly captivating, my senses banging in my ears, drowning out the noise from downstairs. Maybe she'd expired. I'd heard of men who'd drank themselves to death.

It was only when she turned, lashes fluttering, a wee pop escaping from her lips, that I backed out of the room, shutting the door fast behind me. I picked my way downstairs despite the clock on the landing telling me to get a move on. The girls were playing a tag game, falling about, pulling and shoving, a sight I saw as ridiculous.

Amy stood at the kitchen door, her chest rising and falling as if she'd just climbed Ben Lomond.

I said, 'Er, your Mum's sleeping.'

Her eyes widened, the irises so grey they were almost colourless.

I wanted to tell her no to worry, but that would be a bare lie, as opposed to a white lie which was perfectly acceptable in my book, so I planted my feet square in the doorway, stuck two fingers in my mouth and drew out my best whistle. That stilled the melee and I went ower and turned off the record player. All eyes were trained on me; if I didnae act fast this could get out of hand.

I shouted, 'Right you lot. Party's ower. Mrs Roberts is sick. Get your coats and leave. I need to go for the doctor.'

A fox-faced madam sidled to the front of the group, but when I took a step forward and gave her my mother's serpent hiss, she backed off. Within five minutes the place was cleared.

Amy stood at the kitchen door.

'You'll need to tidy up, there's something I forgot,' I said.

Amy sniffed and nodded, her hands shaking, and I hightailed it out of there, changing my shoes at the gate before I took to my sprint.

Outside it was icing up, the ground glowing wi frost. At first my feet were cold in the sannies, but they grew warmer as I ran across Havoc Common, past the empty footbaw fields either side, past the public baths and under the railway bridge. Ower my heid, up in the rafters, invisible pigeons cooed, warbled and fluttered. I sped up when I thought about the white pooh that aye decorated the tunnel's walls and pavements.

I slowed as I reached the East End where the shipyard siren was reaching a crescendo, announcing the end of the shift. The boiler-suited men hadnae yet begun to burst out of the big gates to make their way to the High Street pubs to spend their week's wages, so I was in time. I sped down Victoria Street, the gates now swinging out to empty the tide of working men into the lanes, alleys and streets of the town. Huddles of women, some wi prams, some wi toddlers, some wi curlers under their scarves, waited on the roadsides and pavements ready to relieve their men of their pay packets before too much damage was done. I slid in and out of these clusters, some of them enjoying a good blether, others wan wi cold and anxiety. At last I reached the pre-arranged spot on a corner and waited.

I'd shame him into it if I had to. 'So, we're to starve while you drink our suppers away.' Or 'You're a big man, so you are, taking the food out of the mouths of babes.' I'd heard that one in the chapel. Or, if pushed, I'd resort to wheedling. So far, he'd cooperated but I knew fine and well he still entertained the idea Mum would have him back. Once he realised that wasnae gonna happen, he wouldnae cough up. I stayed in the shadows until I recognised him amongst the crowd. He swaggered whilst others walked, he surveyed whilst others watched, he commanded space whilst others pushed and shoved. As he came closer, a street lamp picked out the pale sweep of his forehead and the glint in his eyes, his oil-blackened lower face split by a grin, and he waved as he located me skulking at the corner. I gritted my teeth as he fell away from the crowd and jogged ower to me.

'How's yer Ma?'

'Fine.' I glanced at his pocket.

'An the weans?' He was going to string this out.

'Aye, fine.'

'Wee Martin?' He bit his upper lip.

'He's getting big.'

'An yersel?'

'Awright.'

He put one hand on the wall and leaned forward, hemming me in. I twisted my heid away and blinked back the sting behind my eyes. He smelt of the yards: Bunsen burner, asbestos, oil, sweat, and that thick peaty undertow that was aye on his breath.

'How's the school?'

'Give's the message.' I slipped under the extended arm and shoved my hand out.

He shook his heid. 'That's ma girl awright, jist aff yer Mam's back.' But he fished out the pay packet, bust it open, took out some notes, and crushed them into his pocket. He passed the still fat packet to me, narrowing his eyes as if about to say something else. Instead he laughed and backed away, soon jogging after his pals.

I turned towards home, jamming the packet in my inside pocket, shivering now, my brain jiving. This time Mum had been to the Social, a lawyer and Father Murphy. Soon as Dad realised the game was up, I'd no be getting any pay packet. Mum said we'd manage, I didnae know how. But it was good to have a calm house for a change, to be able to go to bed and no have to listen for him coming up the stairs garrulous wi the drink. Sometimes after tea, we'd all lie on the carpet and listen to a story on the wireless, as long as Martin was asleep. No, we didnae need Dad or his measly pay packet.

I pushed open the gate and hurried up the path. Mum was waiting in the kitchen doorway, the weans sober-faced at the table behind her. Even Martin's eyes were question marks. I slipped the envelope into Mum's hand and she emptied it onto the sink counter, counting it out.

'Off ye go, Kathleen.' She smiled.

The party? I'd almost forgotten about that. I hesitated. There was one errand left. I slipped into our room and panned beneath my bed for the parcel. It was only a box of Maltesers, a hand-stitched handkerchief I'd made myself, and the glittery birthday card that said *'Happy Birthday Amy'* in my best italics.

1953

Havoc Shore

Ah bolt up the path, past Deid Man's Cave, past the nuns' school an hame tae hide under the stairs in the dark, tae Matt gets in.

Da bangs the front door, thumps by me, sits doon on his chair an bawls fer his tea on the fuckin table. Ah stink but ah'll no come oot tae Matt gets in.

Da sometimes finds me when ah'm hiding. He shouts, Billy-boy come here tae ah clout ye wan, an pulls me oot like a winkle by ma ear. But the day, he cannae be arsed. He curses at oor Betty tae she runs greetin up the stairs. Oor Cathy goes efter her. Ah wish Matt wid get in soon.

Da talks tae hissel. Where's aw the chanty-wrastlers an bastards o this toon, gie em tae me … Where's ma Molly? How come Christ took her an left me wi soddin fools o weans?

He glugs frae the stone jar he gets the whisky in efter it's been stole frae the Bond. Efter a while, it's dunked on the fireplace. When he's snorin ah run up tae ma bed even though ah've no hid ma tea.

Ah goes tae sleep but wakes up. There's bootsteps on the stairs. Ah peek oot. Matt carries oor Betty past ma door, her arms roon his neck, her feet danglin. He shooshes her quiet. He says, it's awright, ah've got ye noo. There's a stink o Da's whisky an his smoke aboot her. Her nightie's tore. The lacy bit hangs doon. Matt's shakin wi the cauld.

He goes intae the lassies' room an ah wait at the door. He lies her doon, covers her up an pits Dolly on the pilla. When he comes oot ah asks him fer a piece. He jist looks at the wall behind me, his face aw crumpled like when he lifted Ma's coffin. Ah tug his jacket an he breathes oot so hard he blows his fringe up frae his forehead. He says, don't go doon the stairs, ah'll bring it up.

But he must've forgot cause he disnae come back.

Ah bum doon the stairs an poke ma nose intae the livin room. The lamp's on, there's big shadows ower the walls. Da's oot fer the coont on his chair. His heid's aw squinty, leanin back, an his eyelids ur like the wings on they dyin flies.

Ah jump when Matt says, Billy-boy get back tae yer bed.

Ah says, but Matt, ah'm starvin.

Da's heid's aw wet. Shiny, like oil's goin doon his hair intae his ear.

Matt says, he's fell an knocked hissel.

Ah says, better get the doctor?

The fire spits an ah jumps mare.

Matt says, nae need. Go get a piece an some milk an go back tae yer bed. Ah'll sit wi him.

Ah goes past Da. His throat creaks. He's aw grey even wi the fire on full bung. Matt says, get on Billy. So ah goes tae the kitchen, switches on the light, takes oot the jam, spreads it on ma piece, bends it so it sticks, gets ma milk an goes past em agin. The scar on Matt's cheek's like butcher's string. He stares at Da like he'd bash him if he moved. The jug aside Da's chair's aw gooey red.

Matt's bashed him awready.

That's how he cannae be goin fer the doctor.

Da's gone quiet.

Ginger's bed's empty.

Ah spill ma milk ower ma haun. Matt looks at the cat's box an shakes his heid. He says, she's lookin fer her kittens.

He gets up, takes ma cup an ma elba, helps me up the stairs. At the top he says, ye saw nothin here the night, understand?

Ah nod, ah unnerston awright.

*

Ma says, clear the decks, quick noo, afore Da comes. Clear the decks or it'll be a skelp on the arse. The plates ur washed an the shoes ur polished an the weans ur tae shut up when he comes in frae his work or else …

Ma rushes aboot the hoose like she's in a race. She says it's a race against time, no enough minutes in the day. She cannae get a breath. Ah rush aboot efter her, under her feet, tae she shouts, Billy. Sit.

Oor Betty tells on me if ah squirm too much. Ma, he's kickin the table, or, Ma, he's rockin agin.

Oor Cathy jist slaps me roon the heid wi her cloth.

Ma shifts ma seat in straight an looks intae ma eyes wi hers wide as the Clyde. She runs her hauns up an doon ma arms tae she rubs ma jitters away.

Matt spars wi me when he gets in. Ah jump up an go *Wheee ho jo* like a Judo fighter an we dae Chinese kicks. Matt goes *Wheee ho jo* back, goes fer ma ears, then ma tum, then ma legs an ah dodge intae his belly, punchin as much as ah can, but it disnae even shift. He's as hard as Ma's washboard. He grabs me an swings me high by ma middle, his fingers diggin intae ma bones so's ah cannae help it, ah squeals. Ah can see doon his throat tae his tonsils, an his big blue eyes ur jist jiggin, so they ur.

Nothin can get me up here, ah'm King o the Castle.

Da bangs the door an sits on the best seat, at the fire, his legs open wide. Ye can smell the Yards aff him, the oil an the sweat an somewhit else steamin aff. Bad temper, Matt says it is, but it's mare like pish tae me. Da sits hunched up. His chin's at his collar an his eyes sink intae they lumpy bags o cheeks but ah'm no fooled, they big hauns ur aye itchin tae smart the skin on boys.

Da disnae say nothin tae Matt. No a word. He jist grunts at him an spits intae the fire, makes it spit back. Matt looks at him sideways ready tae square up, but Da jist grunts noo Matt's big an strong. Matt wid hit him back noo. He widnae let him cut his face agin.

Ma keeps Da away frae me. She gies me the rollin eye tae say yer gettin too loud, Billy. But he'll no hit Ma noo, no since she hid her first heart attack an Matt pushed him against the wall at the hospital, his arm under Da's chin. Da's face wis red as blood an his tongue poked oot tae the doctors came an pulled Matt aff. Noo, even if lumberin aboot on the drink, Da jist curses an grunts at Ma. But he's mean wi the pay packet an she his tae take in washin. She says it's fer extras, like tae pay fer Ginger an oor school stuff.

Ma learns me ma numbers efter the kitchen's cleared cause she says ah'm behind. We sit at the table oot o Da's road. Ma smooths ma hair behind ma ear wi her carbolic fingers, promises me a custard cream if ah get wan right. Gies me wan even if ah dinnae.

*

Teacher keeps eyein me an noddin. Keep at it Billy, you can do it Billy. It's sums, sums, an mare sums. Ah'm tryin tae add up but they never add up right. The clock's tickin ower the class door. Ah watch it but it disnae move. Never mind whit Ma says, time's a slow thing, so it is, specially fer a boy who hates sums.

She's a marvellous woman, Ma says. That Missus McLuskie is a saint, Ma says. An so she is wi they big roon eyes an rosy lips. A pitcher, Matt says. Too bad she's married awready or ah'd ask her masel, he says.

That gied me a fright.

Matt can no way ever get married. Maybe ah could stay wi him an his wife, but then there's Betty. An Cathy. An Ma.

An Ginger. Maybe we could aw go. Leave Da tae clear his ain decks.

Ah looks up at the clock agin an gets anither fright. Cause there's Matt starin at me through the roon windae in the door, like he's no got a body. His eyes ur aw swolled up. Maybe oor Betty's forgot hersel an fell under a bus. Or maybe it's oor Cathy. Naw, she's too clever fer that. Ma heart kicks when ah think it might be Da fell intae the furnace at work, or splashed intae the Clyde an got stuck under a hull.

But Matt widnae be greetin.

Missus McLuskie gets up an goes tae the door an shuts it behind her. Everybody gawps, their mouths open like fish. Ah try tae hear but cannae. Their heads ur both in the glass noo, waverin aboot like they're under the water. The door opens an she slips back in, her big pansy eyes aw wet. She floats ower an takes ma arm, swims me tae the door an Matt gets me roon the chest an sails me doon the corridor an aw the way hame.

*

Matt's been lookin efter us aw summer tae the dark nichts came in, and the leaves aw turned, but he's oot the day cause it's Sunday an that's his day roon at the mates.

Da says tae me, come wi me, you. We've a job tae dae.

Ah dinnae want tae go wi him but ah dinnae want a tannin. He's got his bowls bag an we go doon the hill tae Havoc Shore, me runnin behind him, tryin tae keep up. Ah asks him if ah'm tae get a shot? He laughs at me, the way he does that's no really a laugh, mare like a frog croakin. His face's aw white like he's rubbed it in Vim, an his cheeks've fell in, the bones ur like broken matches.

We pass the nuns' school at Braeside. It looks like a jumble o cardboard boxes on the cliff. An then Deid Man's Cave, where Matt tellt me William Wallace hid afore he got took tae London fer tae be drawn, hung an chopped up. Ah run ma fingers ower the red grit an shiver. Matt aye pits me on his shoulder so's ah can see intae the cave but it's no really much o a cave, mare a slit. Ah know better hiding places than that. William Wallace should've hid me an oor Matt on his side.

We go on doon the path tae where the river passes an the seagulls swoop aboot. There's naebody else alang the water, cause it's wintertime an naebody comes doon here in the winter. It's fair freezin an ah hiv tae pull ma sleeves doon ower ma fingers. Ah looks back up the cliff tae the hooses, wee matchboxes aboot tae tumble ower the edge. The wind tugs like it wants tae pick me up an throw me away.

When we get tae the shore, Da opens the bag an pulls oot a squirmin sack. Ah takes a minute tae get that it's the kittens. The six kittens that Ginger hid an Da disnae like cause they get under his feet. Naebody'll huv em but Matt says it's okay, we'll keep em tae he can find hames. Ah need tae wee an ah must be wrigglin as Da says ah'm tae stop it or ah'll be goin in the fuckin river wi the vermin. Ma chest's sore an ah'm shiverin but ah stay still as ah can. He slips an slides his way doon the bank an ontae the shore, swings the sack high ower the waves tae it sploshes intae the water.

Ah watch fer it tae come up. But it disnae.

The wee soft mouths an the wee noses'll be fillin up an the eyes blinkin in the dark. Warm pee soaks intae ma pants. Da turns, his teeth bitin intae his lip, his nose pinched wi the cauld. No his angry face, mare a look like he's gonna greet. His strands o hair get pulled aw roads by the wind's fingers.

We stand like that fer ages, me peeing masel an him getting wee-er an wee-er, wi the gulls makin circles ower his heid an the wind blowin the long grass aw ways. He drops tae his knees an punches the sky.

Ah bolt up the path, past Deid Man's Cave, past the nuns' school an hame tae hide under the stairs in the dark, tae Matt gets in.

1963

Fox Fur

I kept my head down, pretending interest in the invisible pattern I was tracing on the Formica table. It didnae work. Cathy twisted so she could veer in for a better view of my swollen face.

Her Dusty beehive was so smooth, each strand of copper swept back in a perfect curve, the effect a shining dome. I yanked a lock of dirty blonde behind my ear.

'Still got that keeker on you, Betty. You look a picture,' she said.

I wheezed through the throb in my nose. 'Thanks a lot.'

She sat back, inspection over, but her frown lingered. I ignored that and concentrated instead on the diamond on her engagement ring. It spliced the light as she raised her cup, her rings a stark contrast to the soiled metal of Ma's ring on my wedding finger. Cathy's well-made-up eyes peeked over the cup, her fair lashes black wi mascara. No amount of Panstick could cover my bloated eye.

Considering me like a disapproving headmistress, she crossed her legs and flicked a high heel back and forth, controlled by the flex of her toes. Until it flew off and hit the cooker wi a clang.

'Oh, jeez,' she said, hopping after it.

I swirled sugar into my cup, stray tea leaves circled to the top. I plucked them out wi the base of my spoon.

She sat down again, shoes intact. 'Have a Caramel Wafer.'

She shoved the plate in my face. 'You're thin as a rake.'

What was the matter wi her the night? Wasnae like Cathy to be clumsy. I waited; I'd put my foot in my big mouth too often lately.

She finally spat it out. 'You have to leave Stu, Betty.'

'Got no place to go.'

'There's aye Matt's.' She stifled a snigger and stared down into her tea, eyelashes so clotted wi mascara I wanted to pick it off.

That idea was ridiculous. Matt's house was a tip and I wasnae going to skivvy for him and Billy-boy. Besides, living wi Matt would be suffocating and would mean going back to the auld place. I shivered.

'You'll get something. Council will house you and the weans.'

'No, they willnae.' I was too affronted to tell my big sister about the man from the council, belly hanging over his trousers, fingers tight round my knee. 'They say I can only get the house if Stu agrees. They say I'll make myself homeless. I could even lose the weans.'

'No chance.' She shimmied out of her chair and went to stir the stew; the kitchen heaved wi odours of beef and onions.

'Where's your Harry?' I said.

'Out with his mates. I'll just call the weans in. It's ready, come on, mash the tatties for me. And don't change the subject.' She pursed her lips.

'I'm no leaving Stu. Awright? I just get a bit wound up when he's drinking. I say stuff, then I'm leaving him, but he always changes my mind.' I plunged the masher into her pot.

'Aye, right, but he's not going to get away with using you as a punch bag. Dear God, you'll mash them to mush. I've been thinking, there's only one thing for it.' She hesitated. 'You'll have to come here till he can be made to give up the house.'

'What'll I live on? National Assistance willnae be enough.'

'Right.'

'Anyway, you've no got much room.'

'Aye, right …'

I stopped mashing and added another heel of butter. 'When he's sober, playing wi the weans, stroking their wee heads, wage packet never broke on a Friday …' He always handed it to me wi a kiss. I loved the thickness of the notes, coins heavy in a corner. 'He's a good provider.'

She screwed up her face. 'When he's not plastered.'

Cathy hadnae any idea about a complicated man like Stu, his ways, how his mind worked. I put my shoulder into the mix. She'd no right to judge me; she'd sell her soul for a new handbag. Her clatter around the kitchen assaulted my nerves. Finally, at the top of her voice, she called the weans. My head throbbed.

We sat around the table, my youngest on my knee, and the weans laughed and teased each other silly while I picked at my plate. Occasionally, the wee one rubbed her nose on mine to try to force a smile. Once they were fed, they clambered into the bedroom to play.

Cathy got up. 'We'll go into the living room, leave the dishes till later.'

I followed her through.

'Shut the curtains for me, Betty,' she said, leaning down to turn on a low lamp, her bum heart-shaped in tight linen.

I bit off a fragment of nail and spat it out. The sky was black, streetlights bleached the puddles yellow. I pulled the curtains shut against the sight of bright homes across the street where happy families moved around, folk who had hobbies, and friends who came for their dinners. Cathy had all that. She was sophisticated, my big sister. Stu said, 'Fur coat and nae knickers.' But she'd done well for herself. This was a nice part of Havoc. Good council housing, wide tree-lined streets, on the flat, wi Rennie's corner shop just past the playpark. Good bus connections too.

I listened to my babies giggling wi their cousins in the bedroom. The laughter grew louder when Cathy's Margaret clicked through the lobby wearing a pair of high heels, a pillbox hat that fell over her eyes, and a pure white fur stole. I'd always loved that stole, fastened at the fox's head, but Cathy'd never offered it to me. Course I didnae have anything to go wi it. Cathy tickled the wean all over before chasing her out to more hilarity.

I tried to raise a half-smile, but couldnae stop thinking about Stu. He'd be home from the Yards and starting on the drink, but wi any luck he'd be in a good mood after Wednesday's carry-on. Still, I should've kept my stupid mouth shut. I wished now I hadnae asked him to move his feet off the table.

'It's ma table and ah'll pit ma feet on it if ah like.' He'd scowled, itching for a fight.

'I keep a clean house here, it's no turning into a midden cause you're too lazy to sit right.'

'A midden eh? Jist like yer ma's hoose.'

'Don't you dare ...'

'Gonna get yer big brother ontae me again?'

'That wasnae me,' I said.

'Fuckin wis, ye bitch.'

The fist came out of the air, the floor hit me, I gagged on carpet fibre. He was sorry, wanting cuddles, pressing a facecloth to my nose.

I stubbed out my ciggie and started to rise. 'I'd better be getting on, Cathy. Thanks. That was lovely.'

'No, no. Hold off a wee while yet. The weans are enjoying themselves. Come on, sit down.' She reached over and gripped my arm, so I sat back down.

Cathy's living room was like out of a magazine, wi a gold, velvet three-piece suite. A bar stood in the corner wi some Babycham glasses stacked on a silver tray.

'Harry's making good money. I can let you have a few bob ...'

'It's awright.' I lit up again.

'You've got a good trade, Betty, with the French polishing.' She sat, legs crossed, one hand cupping an elbow, licking her lips like next door's cat.

'Aye, I did have a good trade, but that was when I left school. I was lucky, I suppose ... the one battle Ma won.'

'Me, I wish I'd been allowed a trade. But the buses were awright, before Harry,' she said.

I twisted Ma's ring, looking over at the photo on the mantelpiece, Ma and Da, throttled in their Sunday best. 'He was an auld bastard.'

'He was hard ...but it was the way then.'

'No. It wasnae and it still isnae.' I felt myself colour up, a heat that surged through me, that met the curve of Stu's fist and slammed it back.

'He never laid a finger on us girls, never once,' she said.

God, she really had no idea, or had she locked it away along wi her accent? She thought I didnae know about her elocution lessons. I held her gaze. 'We were scared stiff of him. Battered hell out of the boys. Specially our Billy. Da's work forever on their poor mugs. And have you forgot he hit Ma? Put her in the grave before he went himself.'

'Oh, you can't say that.' Her eyes watered. I'd wrung out some of her satisfaction.

I cranked it up some more. 'He wore Ma down, from noon to night, bringing up us weans, hands raw wi other folk's washing. Waiting on him hand and foot, even after her first heart attack.'

Cathy chewed her lip, leaving a coral smear on her teeth. She knew fine how we used to sit up in bed listening to him call for whisky.

Her face had paled. 'You're right, Betty. Auld bastard.'

She stepped to the fireplace, picked up the photo and laid it face down. 'I'll find one of Ma, instead. Later.'

Cathy bounced back quickly enough, wittering on about the weans, but all I could see was the auld man, hear him effin an blindin, smell the sourness of his breath, the stink of dried-in sweat ... his hands all over me.

Something nipped my palms.

It was her nails. 'Betty?'

'Uh-huh?' The room birled.

'I've got an idea,' she said.

The room came right again. 'How do you mean, an idea?'

'I'm sure Harry's sister would have you for a while. You know, Connie?'

'Connie, in Corby, in England?'

'Yes.'

'England, I havenae been hardly out of the town, never mind England.' I laughed at her but she didnae laugh back. She sat there, intent, on the edge of the couch, her ciggie shedding sparks on the good carpet.

'They're short of skilled workers there. A new boatyard opening up, even taking women workers. Some luxury boatyard on the river near there. Connie'll look after the weans for you too. A lovely person, Betty, and she's family. You need to get away from here. Before ...things could go bad. Think about it. Think of the weans.' She peered at me as if willing me away.

'But Stu's only hit me a couple of times.' I ached for the auld Stu, the man who would've killed anyone who looked at me the wrong way, who once brought me a bunch of daffodils for no reason at all.

She'd had this plan of hers in mind all along knowing I'd never move in wi her. Only asked in the certainty I'd refuse.

The weans had quietened. I found them all fast asleep on Cathy's bed and covered them up, a pity to wake them. When I went back into the living room, Cathy turned on the tele and we watched in shocked silence. President Kennedy'd been shot dead in Dallas. It was all over the news. There was nothing but violence and hate in the world.

Eventually, Cathy kissed me goodnight and I hugged her tight. I packed both my girls into the wee one's pram and pushed them home through the town, past the shipyard, the great cranes disappearing into the night sky over the black belt of the Clyde. Pity they'd shut the local yard. Normally I liked being out at night wi the pram and the wee ones all cosied tight into it, their faces glowing in the streetlights. I felt like I was ten, before it all started, winding home wi my pals when nobody could ever catch me or make me do nothing. But tonight the world felt like a dangerous place. The tenements loomed around me as I picked up pace down Victoria Street.

The door to the flat wasnae locked. I bumped the pram into the lobby, put the brake on and stopped to listen. All was quiet, thank God, though there was a sliver of light under the living room door and the place smelled whisky sour. I lifted the weans, one at a time, settled them in their cots, and kissed their faces, soaking up the silk of them.

I inched open the living room door, intending to cover Stu up, leave him for the night, dampen out the fire and switch off the lights. But dear God in Heaven, the three of them were sprawled like broken sticks across my furniture, Billyboy snoring on the couch and big Matt slumped, dead to the world in the armchair. And my man was out cold beside Billy, blood spattered over his shirt and the start of a right corker of a bruise across his nose. A line of pink slobber trailed from his half-open mouth.

Cathy must've been in on this to keep me so long. In cahoots wi the boys. None of her business. No his either, my fool of a big brother, over here to give Stu another doing. I should've known. Matt who'd promised to look after me. Matt who, the night Da passed, took the weight of my head in his rough hands, and whispered, 'Look after yer ain.' Matt who put me back in my bed while Da moaned on and on. Matt who, in the morning, tellt me Da fell off his chair and split his head on the fireplace and no to worry anymore.

He even believed that himself.

Unable to hold back tears, I closed the living room door and crept towards our bedroom but stumbled over jackets bundled on the floor. Something jabbed my leg. In Matt's pocket, a butcher's knife. My God, Matt up for killing my man, but stopping short at a burst nose. Matt wouldnae know about Corby though, he'd no be having that. Wanted to keep me close. Safe, he called it.

I switched off the hall light and held my breath until I could fumble for the dresser lamp, only to let out a squeal as the face in the mirror leapt towards me. Swollen, tear-stained, one eye puffed and discoloured, the mouth slack. It was Ma. 'No use greetin an girnin, girl,' she mouthed, but when I dabbed my eyes wi the edge of my sleeve, I saw only the wreck of my own face. I grabbed my ring finger and twisted off the wedding band, dropped it onto the dresser and watched it spin to a stop.

1963

Ring of Fire

We were in a corner of the pub, our backs tae the wall, so we could keep an eye on the bar and the front door for unwelcome company. The Cutty was awready filling up, be heaving later when Friday's backshift came out the Clydebank yards, but even now smoke sat like fog at eye level. I lit another fag, took a draw, added tae the ambience.

On the turntable, Johnny was gien it laldy wi his *Ring of Fire*.

Beside me, Billy-boy swallowed gulps of air, his Adam's apple a minnow in a net. He needed something tae get on wi. Another hauf hour would dae it, just tae the night drew in and folk closed their curtains. We were getting looks from one of the regular clientele. I mouthed at him tae fuck off and the nosey git spun back tae the bar.

'Get another round in.' I shoved a ten-bob note at Billy.

He crackled it in his fist. 'Aye Matt, nae bother big man, right away.' He knocked the table as he went.

I blew ash from my sleeve as Billy shouldered between two punters, patted the note down, then elbows digging the bar, took tae his rocking.

'Ye awright, Son?' McLeish mouthed, wiping a glass wi his filthy cloth.

I leant forward, ready tae break up the niceties. My wee brother was on a guarantee of a sore heid if he breathed a word about our Betty.

'Aye, nae bother. How's yous?' Billy shouted.

I sat back. Shook my heid. When I was in the lobby pulling on my coat, Billy had breenged out of the scullery wi The Record. 'Whit ye dain wi that,' I said, knowing fine he never read nothing. When I grabbed it, a knife clattered ontae the linoleum. 'Whit's that for?'

'Jist in case, Matt.'

'Put it back in the fuckin drawer.'

'Aye, aye, awright.' He'd sloped off.

I stubbed out my fag, breathed nice and slow, cracked my knuckles, splayed my fingers. Black nails, a welder's trademark. A Swarfega bath would sort that and I'd be a fine boy for the Palais the morrow night. The ladies aw said I was Johnny Cash's double. I'd show they gals a ring of fire awright. Dress masel up in my teddy boy gear. Och, well maybe no. Nae chance of a lumber wi Billy-boy on my tail.

I flicked a bar mat round and round. Da's watch caught a stab of light from the bare bulb. He used tae sit here, pontificating tae aw and sundry, wi his rusty one-liners, 'Yer a scholar and a gentleman', his shag tin in front of him, a hauf and a hauf neat at his hand, the gold watch gleaming. My watch. Mine by right of succession. I'd lifted that stiff wrist, inched the bracelet free and slipped it off. Cold fingers ran up my spine. I straightened my back, rolled my shoulders.

'A hauf an a hauf, Big Man.' Billy-boy slid the tray on the table. How he'd got across the floor, who the fuck knew, but now the beer was slopping ower the lip.

'Jesus, a cardinal sin, Son.' I swiped the drips from my glass and downed the cold brew through the froth.

He laughed. 'Where wis yous jist then?' He took a slurp of his pale ale.

'I was thinkin of Da, if ye must know.'

'Aye?' His eyes narrowed and he jumped as if expecting the auld man tae appear in the bar.

'Aye.' I looked away.

Drumming his fingers on the table, he said, 'He was a hard man hissel. But wisnae it fast at the end? Jist fallin aff his chair like that.'

We both knew the auld man hadnae just fell off his chair. Cause of death: *accident while inebriated*. Well, near enough. Course, Billy might've forgot that night. Ten years was a lifetime tae him. I wondered how he got on at his work, specially in the butcher's line where a steady hand was needed. He was fidgeting wi the bar mat now, dunting it on the table tae *I walk the Line*.

'Sit at peace, Son. Yer doin my heid in. Folk'll think we're up tae something.' I moved tae grip his fingers. They retreated up his sleeve. It was like trying tae get a hold of a crab skittering on the sand at Havoc Shore. Had some guid days down there as weans. Sunny days when Da was hissel, he'd haul me up tae his shoulders and run me intae the Clyde, my thighs bumping off his chest. We'd walk back slow, trailing between the jellyfish glistening on the sand. They looked saft but could gie ye a mighty sting. It came tae me that Billy-boy hadnae known Da when he was awright, before the drink took his wits.

Billy was elbowing me. 'We ur up tae something,' he whispered, loud enough tae bring in the polis. Though a blind eye'd be turned if they knew our business.

'Just a genteel reminder so he gets the message.'

'But he didnae get it the first time.' He peered at me ower his glass wi they great blue eyes.

'Reinforcement,' I said slow as I could.

'Whit's that?'

'Did they no teach ye nothing at that special school?'

'Naw. Well, aye and naw. No big words like that.' He took a gulp of his beer. 'Matt?'

'Whit?' I spat. He was getting on my wick.

'Ah think we should gie him a bigger fright.'

'Fuck sake.' Johnny Cash was for bringing his guns tae

town right this minute trained on Billy-boy. Had I no gone ower this wi him before we came out? Stu would get whit he gied Betty, and a bit more. Nobody got away wi hurting my wee sister.

I pulled the glass from his hand and set it down. The bar quietened, ears pricked as the song faded. I caught the barman's eye; gied him the nod. Business. He turned tae serve a punter. The bar stirred again. I downed the dregs of my beer and shoved Billy's glass tae the other side of the table. His hand shot out like we were in the fuckin desert, then wi the ale still streaming down his chin, I twisted him out by the collar intae the pishin rain.

We were soaked by the time we got tae Betty's flat, just up the road from the shipyards, used tae be noisy in the day wi the clanging of the works, quieter now, but it was a guid close wi decent neighbours. The trouble was inside it. Stu peered round the door, chain on, keeping us dripping on the landing. His lashes were long like a lassie's. I wanted tae shoot my fist in and plug him right there and then. He looked us up and down. 'She's no in, her an the weans are at yer Cathy's.'

Course they were. Cathy had seen tae it that her man was out the night so that Betty could come round for a sisterly chat. 'We're here tae see you, Stu.' I stared at him through the gap tae a tic took hold in his eye. He flicked the chain and opened the door just enough tae let us pass. Billy's feet tangled wi mine, near upending me.

I ditched my coat in a corner of the lobby and reached out for Billy's. He turned away, pulling it close. 'Fuck sake, gies yer jacket.' I tugged, but he shrugged me off, face screwed up like a bull terrier's.

The coals glowed red in the living room grate. The only other light, a sick yellow, came from a low lamp beside the couch. I stepped tae the window. A mongrel zigzagged up the road, lifted its leg, pished on the lamppost, then tripped on up the street, turning sharp round the corner. Billy was aye asking for a kitten, he was wearing me down. Maybe a puppy … Two fellas ponced by, hair flicked back, Brylcreem shiny under the lamp. Teddy boy suits wi big lapels out on the town. Lucky buggers. The night ate them up.

I shut the curtains and swung round. Billy-boy sat on the edge of an armchair, a can of McEwan's at his feet. He lit up a fag, its tip glowing like a tiny furnace. I shifted, uneasy. Wasnae sure about this … but I was sure now I shouldnae have brought Billy. He might be nearing twenty but he was a disability in a crisis.

'So Matt, whit brings ye here this fine evenin?' Stu sat down on the couch, crossed his legs.

Fine evening, my arse. 'I think ye know why I've had tae come here again.'

He was smooth, I'd gie him that. He sat there, a lace doyley at his heid, a fuckin halo, studying me, like I was something out a zoo. Most folk wouldnae dare dae that. Da's mark was on me and it scared the shit out of them.

'No idea at aw, Matt. No a clue.' He extended both hands in a question and tried tae stare me out.

I didnae like that one bit. Billy didnae like it one bit. He was off the seat and at Stu before I could yank him off. 'Ye bastard. Ah'll slit yer fuckin throat,' he shouted, his face beet.

Jesus, I hoped he wasnae going intae one of his fits. Stu was laughing as he squirmed off the chair, Billy hanging on. They circled like two skinny Sumo wrestlers. I sobered masel, grabbed Billy's sodden jacket, got my arm around his trunk, the stench of sweat hitting me like a punch tae the nose; there it was, the steel sliding out of his pocket. I stuck the cold blade back in, heat flaring down my spine.

Thank Christ, Stu didnae look like he'd noticed. Too busy smirking. 'Yer sister's no aw she's cracked up tae be, yer wee brother needs tae be put back on the leash,' he said.

Swallowing bile, I patted Billy's cheeks. 'Awright, Son?'

He blinked and squeezed his eyes tae they focused. 'Aye, aye, Matt …jist lost it a bit there.'

I wished he really was awright, then maybe he'd get hissel a lassie and I'd get some peace. Sometimes I'd go intae his room when he was sleeping and he looked like a wee angel, face relaxed and hair falling like straw ower his foreheid.

Shaking my heid, I shrugged the anorak from Billy's shoulders, went intae the lobby, shifted the knife tae my ain pocket, and let the jackets slump on the floor away from Betty's flowery wallpaper. Reminded masel why we were here, tellt masel tae play it cool, rubbed my hands thegither tae stop the trembling.

'Want a hauf?' This from the wanker in the living room.

'Aye.' I needed one badly if I was going tae get this job done clean.

Billy piped up, 'Me tae.'

'Ye've had enough.' I sat down in the other armchair.

He sank back.

'A foreman noo ah hear, Matt.' The eejit poured two slugs of whisky. 'Water?'

'That's for sailing boats in.'

He laughed, aw pally. 'Yer jist like yer Da, jist aff the auld man's back.' He handed me my nip, flopped back down and watched me.

My whisky went down slow, lining my throat wi fire. I peeked at Billy hunched up in his seat. He'd gied hissel a fright. Flash Stu sat, knees crossed, relaxed, looking like that Paul Newman. Except he kept scratching his fingers up and down the arm of the couch.

'So ye're a foreman noo, Matt.'

'I'm no deaf, I heard ye the first time.' I was proud tae be the gaffer, had a heid for getting the job done. Had a guid job at John Brown's in Clydebank. But I wasnae looking for compliments from this dunderheid. 'Whit d'ye mean she's no aw she's cracked up tae be?'

Stu looked at me like a man in mourning. 'She's got a gob on her.' He crossed and uncrossed his legs.

Gied it a few seconds, then I said, 'Our Cathy's got a gob on her. Betty's saft as shite.'

He was warming tae his ain claptrap. 'Thinks she can tell me whit tae dae in ma ain house.'

I said nothing. Let him hang hissel.

'But there's worse.' He hesitated, the sure sign of a liar. 'She's got a fancy man.'

Billy-boy giggled. I got up and moved towards Stu wi they menaces.

'Ah swear it,' he squeaked as I gripped his oily neck. Then he backtracked. 'Ah'm no saying anything's goin on, no yet, just some geezer gien her the eye. Ah didnae hit her Matt, honest. Ah shoved her, jist a wee bit, she fell. Knocked hersel on the table there. Look, see.'

I let go of his neck, clutching his collar as I turned. Right enough, it was possible ... and Betty was a guid looking woman, wi that pile of blonde hair and her bonny smile. Many a fella in the town had the eye on her.

One time I came home, no long before the auld man passed, and she was swanking up and down the living room wi a pair of high heels she'd got out a jumble sale, wi her school uniform and ankle socks, like a bag of bones Marilyn Munroe. Da came in. 'Fuckin whore,' he croaked, setting her eyes alight. Those eyes hadnae been the same since Da died. Like a candle had been thumbed out.

Stu was making a noise. 'Matt ...' he said, and I moved. A crack, the nose squelched. His hands came up, splayed ower his face. Blood splattered his fingers like rain.

I wished I hadnae punched him so hard, beside the fact my knuckles ached. No that he didnae deserve it, just that it was aye me had tae finish things. I tellt him tae get a dishcloth.

He ran it under the kitchen tap, and I made him sit wi it clamped tae his face, heid back. Billy-boy was muttering stuff, his voice whining like steel on steel.

Stu spurted, 'Christ Matt, ah think ma nose is broke.'

That riled me and I wanted tae bust it again but I stepped back. The sissy was greetin, a gluey puddle settling at the corner of his mouth. That slowed me, and I looked down at my hands, at the watch, and it was like I was crumbling tae ash inside. Fuck sake, surely there were better ways tae fix things than this. I poured Stu a drink, relented and let Billy have one too, refilled my ain tumbler, and turned on the tele. I scratched my nail down the ridge on my left cheek.

Da got whit he deserved but it should've been me, no wee Betty standing ower his chair staring intae the fire that last night, the heavy jug limp in her hand, Da slumped, heid at his knees. I'd prised the neck from her fingers, laid the jug on the floor, checking her front. Clean. Hefted her up, heid tucked under my chin, the back of her neck silted wi hair and sweat, and slipped her intae bed. Aw the time white hot under my skin. Keeping it in check, making sure our Cathy didnae wake up.

I fed Stu enough whisky tae fell him. Billy and me watched some crap film till the news came on. Kennedy had been assassinated in America. Shot in his limousine. Should've had the lid on it, eejit. Might no have been his fault. They security fellas should've made sure he was awright. Too bad. I liked Kennedy. I had tae wait till Betty came in, tae explain masel. Cathy was tae keep her back tae late but it was nearing midnight. We fell asleep and when morning broke, I shook Billy awake and padded intae the lobby, so's no tae disturb Betty and the weans. The bedroom door was shut fast. I wanted tae talk wi her so bad acid seared my stomach. Nearly knocked on the door, but she'd be pissed if I woke the weans. Instead, I turned away and lifted our jackets off the pegs where she'd hung them tidy like. We left

Stu snoring like a train.

On the Monday I reported tae the boss. She gied me grief.

'Fuck sake, Cathy, least I done the job. I can hold my heid up. Stu's got a keeker that tells everyone whit he is.'

'Aye right, you're a big man, so you are. What about our Billy, another fit?'

'Och, the doctor'll sort out his pills this morning. Must've fell off a wall when he was wee.'

She rolled her eyes, crossed her silky legs. Clammed up tight about our Betty. Face like a pan loaf. Would only say she was safe and a letter would come sometime.

'Stu deserved it, he had the gall tae try tae blame our wee Betty for him smackin her around. Said she drove him tae it wi her wiles. I'll no have anythin bad said about her. Look after yer ain. Right?' I said.

'As you've always done.'

'Aye, aye.' I didnae want tae cross her. But … I needed tae make sure Betty was awright. 'Come on Cathy, where is she? She could've come tae me. I'd have taken her in, if it was that bad.'

But at least Betty knew whit I'd done for her that last night. I'd watched Da for hours. He woke up a couple of times, blood rippling in the bristle on his chin. He muttered, called out. I weighed it aw up, waited till I was sure, then dragged him off his seat like a sack of spuds, placed him so the crack in his scalp was on the grate. Went tae my bed, smoked the rest of the night away. When I got up for work he was ice-cold. He looked thinner, whiter, less creased, more like my Da.

Cathy stared out at the rain, but I went on, 'Could dae wi a bit of help around the auld place. Billy-boy's no much of a cook even if he knows how tae slice a steak.' The lump in my throat threatened tae choke me.

Smoke rings angled by my heid.

I sat a bit longer, then thumbed out my fag and stood up.

I looked around. 'Ye've got this place nice, Hen.'

Chucked some change on the table for the weans. Gied her the nod.

Some things are too broke tae fix.

1963

The Midden

The rain battered the windows with the rat-tat-tat of a machine gun. Matt sat next to the fireplace, his work clothes reeking oil, steam rising from one trouser leg with the whiff of burning tar. I'd hoped he wouldn't bother, leave me out of it, but he was after something. I knew what, of course, but I hadn't expected him to leave the Yards at lunchtime to come to see me. Specially in this rain. I crossed my legs, smoothed my nylons, pursed my lips, pretending no to be too happy about his antics on Friday.

'Fuck sake, Cathy, least I done the job. I can hold ma heid up. Stu's got a keeker that tells everyone whit he is.'

Thank Christ he was on a hard seat and no my new couch. I'd have made him come in the kitchen but he'd disturbed me at the wringer and that was a tangle of bedding and knickers. Bedding and knickers that needed drying on the pulley cause of the rain. I ushered him into the living room, keeping well back from the possibility of my skin near that rough boiler suit, or worse, getting a blast of welder sweat that might bring up my breakfast.

'Aye, right, you're a big man, so you are.'

It didn't take guts to threaten the likes of Stu, especially when there were two of you. But Matt was never great on sarcasm. This went in one ear and swirled about his empty head as the rain pummelled the roof.

'Stu deserved it, he had the gall tae try tae blame our wee

Betty for him smackin her around. Said she drove him tae it wi her wiles. I'll no have anythin bad said about her. Look after yer ain. Right?' He thumped his knee to drive the point home.

I'd reduced that man of Betty's on first sight. The cheek of him: the shock of his hand on the swell of my hip and the little slap he thought was going to get me to shag him. I threw my gin and bitter lemon into his face, smiling as his front teeth nicked his lip scarlet. He could do nothing but take out his grubby hanky to dab at the blood.

'As we've always done,' I said.

'Aye, aye. Ye know I'd dae anythin for you lassies. Might take me longer tae get there but I'll aye finish a job, nae loose ends.'

I knew exactly how far he'd go.

He put on his crooked grin, the one he thought worked wonders with the ladies. He was a fine boy, dark curls and they long-lashed baby blue eyes, even the scar on his left cheek added a bit of mystery to a man who was straight as a plank. 'Come on Cathy, where is she? She could've come tae me. I'd've taken her in, if it was that bad.' His voice splintered. 'She's my sister, as well.'

I turned away, made as if I was watching something fascinating out the window, though all I could see was rain blasting the glass in never-ending streams. Matt near to greetin?

He tried again. 'Could dae wi a bit of help around the auld place. Billy's no much of a cook.'

The auld place? Matt and Billy weren't much good at cleaning either. A midden to this day. Da's seat still there by the fire, though the earthenware jug of whisky that sat at his feet was long gone. The stink of drink and the foostiness of drying overalls came back to me as did Ma's laundry in the scullery, crisscrossing the room. And damp that filled your nose, your lugs, your mouth. We always had the snuffles in that house.

Matt was giving me a sore head, pain pulsed at my temple. I rubbed it away. I'd tell him where she was, aye, in my own good time. I tried to distract him. 'How's the work going?'

'Och, awright. Got the afternoon off. Said Betty wasnae well again.'

Matt gave a miserable wee laugh. We both knew the lie in that. It wasn't funny. Da had left his mark on Betty as sure as he had that puckered seam on Matt. I touched that one time, just after Ma died, when he was tucking Betty into bed beside me. I leaned over and ran my finger down his face. On his smooth cheek there was a series of bumps, like when I darned a blouse. 'Is it sore?'

'Naw, jist itchy sometimes.' He threw the covers over our heads and we giggled.

Now, he looked around. 'Ye've got this place nice, Hen.' He nodded at the bar in the corner. Out of his league, special purchase from Macdonald's in Glasgow. Padded red leatherette and a stack of Babycham glasses twinkling on the counter. I sighed. Matt couldn't sit in a room with liquor without licking his lips.

He sat on a bit longer, gabbing about his work, how the gaffers hadn't a clue, no news there, then he pretended he knew something about the world. 'Kennedy shot, eh?' he said as he thumbed out his doup and unwound his long frame. Nodded in a deliberate way as if he'd come to a decision. I waited but he declined to share. He looked in the mirror at his best side, fumbled into his pockets for change. 'For the wee lassies,' he said, dropping sixpenny bits on the coffee table. One landed on its rim and spun, only stopping as the front door banged close.

I squeaked a space clear in the windowpane. He breenged down the street, slowing to snap a drooping twig from one of the trees lining the avenue, one that the high winds had caught last night. He finished the job, chucking it away at his feet. What you saw was what you got with Matt. He gripped the world in both big fists.

In the kitchen, fat spools of wet bedding, fresh from the wringer, waited to be hung up. I set the basket on the table, unwound the rope from its figure-of-eight hook and let the pulley squeal down to chest height, making sure it was level, tying the rope fast. Bad bloody weather, even for November, no chance of drying on the green. Dampness coated everything. When it wasn't wet it was freezing. Enough to turn sheets stiff as corpses on the washing line. You had to punch them into shape. These ones were still warm as I began to hang them up on the pulley, aggravated by the spoiling of my kitchen, turned into a washerwoman's hovel. Just like Ma's.

I ran my fingertips over the Formica worktop, the smooth expense of it making me smile. Harry and I had done well for ourselves. We were going up in the world. The house was already better than the neighbours' or any of my friends'. Even if it was a council house. I took particular satisfaction from the naked envy on Betty's face on Friday night.

At first I thought all my plans had been for nothing. Betty always made excuses for Stu's temper, but I was relieved when on Friday she returned with the girls fast asleep in the pram, within the hour, her case packed. Whatever it was that changed Betty's mind in the end, I didn't know, but finding her two brothers and her man fast asleep in her living room while she stood with a keeker the size of your palm would be enough to make anybody do a runner. Specially when your man's nose was dripping blood.

Gripping a peg between my teeth, I flapped out a sheet, folded it over a slat and pinned it tight. It was badly crinkled, the bugger, and I stretched it into shape. I picked up one corner and doubled it back, reducing the length of the hang.

Betty was gorgeous, even though I still thought of her as my wee sister, thumb sooked scarlet, they big misty eyes.

Mind, she might as well have 'gie me a leathering' stamped on her forehead, she looked so bloody helpless. It was the pallor of her skin, the veins strung like tributaries in the cream of her skin, temple to throat. The way she seemed to fold in on herself at the least wee thing. She'd be awright in Corby. Harry's sister would look after her until she got on her feet. Nothing more to worry about.

Tears welled as I bent to retrieve a pillowcase. I sniffed them away, closed my eyes tight, instead allowing gall to rise. Bastard got what he deserved, Matt saw to that and I fixed the rest.

Halfway to the pulley I halted, my chest tightening. I wasn't going to let the what-ifs take hold. Fill yer heid wi plans, pleasant thoughts, like the new stuff ordered from the catalogue, they warm liberty bodices for the weans, yer new black silk suspenders. Think of the balance written in blue ink on yer bankbook. Dinnae think about Da.

I slumped down, shoved the basket away, lit up, fingers shaking.

Betty couldn't stay in this town. She could bring us all down, might blabber. Once she remembered. Less chance in a new place surrounded by new people.

A brother who was a fuckin murderer would ruin everything.

The court case, the headlines, the tittering behind curtains. The sin would spread, taint us all. And worse. Matt could hang. Betty would shatter.

Vomit burst into my mouth and I shuddered to the sink. The stink of it made me grue again and another pile gorged my mouth. I spat it all out, and hands shaking, wiped my face. My stomach was hollow so I circled my palm over my belly till it calmed, still seeing Matt walk to his end in Barlinnie Goal, his head down as they put the noose around his neck. There were stories. How a man could swing, his neck failing to break. He'd strangle to death, legs flailing high for minutes. *For Chrissake, Cathy, yer getting hysterical. Calm doon.* I shook the Vim over the sink, squeezed the mess down the drain and threw away the cloth.

Da had been cleaned up, awright. Matt told the story to the police and the doctor and never departed from it. No that I blamed him. Far from it. Wished I had the guts myself. I was too young then. Instead I wished a hundred million deaths on Da. He never touched me. Never. He never had. Someone was keening, the noise barely detectable under the crashing rain. I stapped my mouth shut. But he touched Betty. Course, I was older and Betty was Betty, glaikit.

That time, me traipsing downstairs looking for her, after I turned onto the cold bedsheet beside me. Picking my way down the stairs in the yellow glow of the street lamp, my toes curling on the ice of the linoleum, heart thumping as I turned the corner.

Firelit shadows always dart around the walls. Da fills his chair, the jug stolid at his side, grey head tipped back, mouth open, crimson tongue poking out, eyes slits. Betty's on the armrest in her nightie, her white legs parted, the hem ridden up, staring across the room. Da's hand skitters across her thigh to his lap. He dunts her on the back, she stands up, sways. He grunts – 'Och, take the silly thing back tae her bed, she's jist come doon here tae annoy me.' Betty's hand slip-slides in mine, I lead her upstairs, tuck her in, his whisky-sweat on her.

I could've been havering.

But why did I always go back and smooth down her nightie and make it so she wasn't on his armrest but on the other chair? Like in a dream, how sometimes you rearranged the story while you were still asleep if you didn't like how it was going.

That last day, me and Betty going up early to keep out Da's road. Matt away with his mates. Billy hiding in his usual place under the stair. Me, falling asleep when I guess the auld man will have dozed off. Then waking with a start, the bed frozen beside me. Matt coming in with Betty in his arms and laying her down, her nightie torn, the lacy bit free. Matt's rough whispers. Billy's wailing. The disgust lined on Matt's face.

The next day Da's dead.

Matt cool, acting all grief-stricken, friendly with the doctor and the policeman. Pats on the back, murmurs of consolation. All that Da had been packed away in the coffin, like a drawer full of foosty strips of bedding. And he became somebody else. A poor auld soul who'd lost his wife and then went downhill with the drink. His swearing, his fists, his bristled cheeks, his putrid stink buried with him.

I wondered if I was making too much of it. But it was deep in Betty's eyes. That lost look, those blank moments. Matt must've found out and he wouldn't have stood for it. Everyone has their breaking point and that was Matt's. Da could hit him or us and he wouldn't have liked it, might've hit the auld bastard but this? No, Matt killed Da that night cause of Betty. Bashed him with his own jug. I worked it all out that morning. The jug was on the kitchen drainer. Washed, empty. There was a crack running from the lip to base that was new. I knew that jug like the back of my hand. A cracked skull on the fireplace? My arse. It was Matt. He came home and saw what I saw that last time. Or worse, Betty naked up to the waist and Da's filthy hands all over her, cold and doughy except for the hard pads on his palm, and Matt lost it. Pulled her off and picked up the jug and let him have it. Wouldn't be any fight. Da was always pissed. The shock on the auld man's face, Betty fainting, all six-foot-two of Matt towering over the chair. The dregs of whisky puddled on the floor. A smell too, blood, grime and that distillery yeasty stink.

One day Betty might talk. Even if I was havering, she was best away from Stu, a new life. This was the right thing.

Something kept flitting back as I filled the pulley. Something off-kilter. Big eejit Matt? Matt sitting here this morning near greetin? A plain man, straight as a plank. The jug wasn't really his style.

Matt hadn't enough guile to pick up a jug and bash the auld man. Matt, who gripped the world in two big fists. Matt would've punched him to a pulp.

I stumbled back, leant heavily on the table, dropped a sheet. Could it have been an accident after all? I laughed out loud. At my own stupidity, all these ten years I thought Matt had killed Da.

As if that could've happened. Matt would've let on. And he'd never said a word.

I'd go see Matt the morrow with Betty's address. Maybe give that midden of his a good clean.

The pulley secured, I went to the toilet, threw cold water over my face and got out my make-up bag. I redid the foundation, making sure there weren't any streaks, padded powder over my cheeks, added a bit of blusher to highlight my cheekbones. Applied some dark eyeliner, blue shadow and a coral lipstick. The bus was due at the mill dam, and now that the rain was a soft drizzle, I could have a nice stroll up the High Street before picking up the girls for our elocution lesson.

1963

Trip Switch

Fergus thumbed out another doup, tossed it in the litter can at the borstal's porch, ventured a few yards up the brae tae the corner and scanned the road. Nothing. He straightened his uniform jacket, pulled down the cuffs of his shirtsleeves, and checked his watch. The fags hadnae shifted the sour taste he had in his mouth since taking the phone call after the special hearing at the High Court. This was a bad case for The Vinel. Half an hour should be enough for them tae get here on a Saturday morning. Where the hell were they?

It was bad news weekend. Kennedy shot tae death in Dallas right in front of the wife, and those FBI men loping helpless at the side of the limousine.

Somebody wasnae doing his job, that was for sure.

Fergus was about tae take out his fags again when a van crunched its way down the drive and rumbled tae a stop. Keeping a close eye on its occupants, he secured the Borstal door open wi the wooden stop. A scurry, a yelp, and a skelf of a lad was bundled out, shoulders making tae clout the guards at every turn.

The aulder Uniform, hands like shovels, thrust papers at Fergus's chest. 'No pretty reading, better watch yersel. Tae next hearing. Three weeks.'

'Nae cuffs here.' Fergus's gander rose at the man and his pronouncements.

'When he's ower the threshold.' The guard prodded his

delivery ower the step and the boy stumbled. Fergus moved tae steady him, only tae be shaken off. A crack of cuffs and the Uniforms lumbered back tae their van.

Wide arses in fat jobs.

Fergus toed away the doorstop and let the door sigh shut. The boy was wire tense. Fergus inched close, just enough tae see the fine web of hair on the lad's nape, and the bloom of blue at his temple. The boy's eyelashes flickered as his head dipped. A weak ray of sunlight caught a droplet mid-lash, which might have become a tear if it hadnae melted away wi a blink. Fergus almost reached out tae touch the boy's sleeve, tae reassure him, but the pulse in the thin neck told him tae stay back. He held his breath, clutched at the keys in his pocket and let his body inch forward, worried any sudden movement might trip a switch. Two steps forward and the boy stirred behind him, plimsolls squeaking as he followed Fergus along the corridor tae the back of the building until they reached the dormitory. Fergus fingered the keys out of his pocket. He slid one intae the keyhole, a turn, a pop, holding the door tae his chest, knee controlling the velocity, pushing it open an inch at a time until it widened tae display the dorm. It was smaller than the rest wi only two sets of bunks, four lockers, a central dome of a light and a high window. A bundle of clothing sat middle of a lower bunk.

Fergus sloped tae the far wall, allowing the boy a clear view. He raised his arms, palms outward tae invite the lad in, aware of eyelids pale as crescent moons, of shoulders bent as if water could slough right off them.

'Ah'll leave ye here,' he said. 'Ye'll no share this room. Call me Mr Machrie. Ah've sorted out some gear for ye. A senior boy'll come and show ye the ropes. If ye need me later, ah'll be around.'

He left in bad need of a drink and a fag.

He'd never been much of a drinking man, but he'd like tae clear the taste of boak circling his mouth. And shift the sight of his auld pal Paddy Donnelly's coffin on the shoulders of his uncles, carried down Church Road, Mister Donnelly so shaken he was barely able tae walk behind them.

He hadnae thought of that for years.

For the rest of the day, and the next, the boy kept himself tae himself. Everybody else kept out of his way. Once or twice, Fergus passed a remark, but the boy aye moved his arse. Fergus wanted tae give him a good shake, tell him tae buck up. But he knew those tactics never worked. He'd find another way.

He wasnae one tae give up on any boy, no matter what he'd done.

An opportunity came during the games' session. The boy stood alone at the side of the playing field, staring at the match.

'No want tae have a go?'

The boy pinned Fergus's gaze, challenging him.

Fergus looked away.

A twist of boot lifted turf before the boy swaggered down the line. Fergus's jaw tightened as the lad veered off tae the class block. He almost jogged after him tae haul him back by the neck.

But it wasnae worth making a fuss about.

He let it go.

At breakfast on the third day, one of the younger residents, Andrew Carr, seventeen going on seven, swaggered up tae the boy as he ate alone at the table furthest from the counter. Dolly, the cook, looked up open-mouthed from her ladling, face flushed under her soot black hair and nodded tae Fergus in warning.

The clodhopper scratched away the seat, slumped down across from the boy, elbow ower the back of the chair, swinging to and fro. The boy's head was set fast tae the window, at the wall of the latrines. Carr opened wi a gaffe. 'So, wee man, whit ye in fer?'

When this didnae merit a reply, Carr stood up and moved closer on his tree trunk thighs. His breathing became loud wi the effort of standing still.

The room folded in, like a soaked cardboard box.

Fergus's thigh muscles tensed.

The boy didnae shift.

Carr swung around tae face his pals, his grin bursting like bubblegum when he saw the drooping heads, heard the shuffling feet. Picking up their signals at last, he swivelled back tae the boy who was now rising from his seat, eyes smouldering, a pulse beating at his temple.

Fergus moved. He gripped Carr by the collar and jerked him back, enough tae begin what soon became a willing slide back tae his mates.

'Keep him here.' He nodded tae one of the lads.

'Nae bother, Mr Machrie.' The lad gripped his pal by the sleeve.

Having dumped Carr, Fergus shifted his weight tae the other leg and dipped towards the boy. He looked intae eyes that glistened wi menace before the whites slanted away. The boy sank back down, awready switched off.

Fergus sat back in his seat, the canteen stirred, Dolly flicked the tea towel, pursed her lips, and raised five fingers. He took a deep breath, slowing the thrum of his heart.

She joined him a few moments after the trill of the class bell.

'Close one, Fergie, Son.'

He flinched but kept shtum. Nobody got tae call him son anymore, but she had the privilege of age. And the privilege of kin, being his wife's aunt.

'Aye,' he allowed. He lit up, petrol teasing his nostrils.

'Plenty talk goin on.'

He shook his head. She'd consulted her register of births, marriages and deaths, and the special file wi aw Havoc's gossip. 'Expect so.'

'Ye look a bit worried yersel, Son.'

'No me.'

'Dinnae kid a kidder.' Her eyes seared him tae his seat. He needed tae offer her something. Otherwise, she'd keep drilling.

'He's a powder keg, right enough,' he said.

'Bad choice of words.' She tilted her jet-black beehive.

He could never work out how the hell that creation defied gravity.

She said, 'Getting younger every year. Whit's he, fifteen?'

'Fourteen.'

'When's the trial?'

'Three weeks. Shouldnae be here. We're no Remand.'

'We're whitever the courts say we are.' She took a drag, puckered her cherry lips, deepening the herringbone lines around her mouth. 'It's no like you, but.'

'What?'

She stilled, elbow on the table, smoke curling past her ear. He felt the lash before the sting. 'Tae be actin like a big feartie.'

A flush seared his neck and cheeks. He stubbed out his fag and plonked his hands under the table tae steady them. 'C'mon Dolly, ah'm no feart of a wee boy.'

She stood up and stroked his arm. 'Ah didnae say that.' She padded away, lifted the counter flap, and disappeared intae her kitchen.

He left the canteen, snatched his scarf and jacket from the peg behind the office door, and murmured tae the boss that he'd be back in a bit. The bite of the Clyde's arctic blast would clear his mind.

He strode the road downhill tae the bridge against a thief of a wind, stopping for his newspaper at the tobacconist's, the counter still covered wi pictures of the Kennedy assassination, aw saying Ruby would fry.

Which was awright wi Fergus. Let the bastard sizzle. He

had no right tae take matters intae his own hands.

After folding his *Daily Record* intae his jacket wi the ten-pack of Capstans, he darted across the road tae take the Elvern's path. Approaching the palings at the tumbling water he felt for his lighter, teased the packet from his chest pocket, fished out a fag, tickled it between top teeth and tongue and bent his body, giving shelter tae the spurt of flame. His hands quivered and the bugger needed reigniting three times before the tip took a glow. He puffed till it had life enough tae take the slate of the wind.

Aye, this boy was getting tae him awright.

But any attempt tae approach was met by flint. Those eyes were aye scanning the ground except when cornered. Then they sparked alight. But that was aw outside bravado. He'd seen plenty of that before.

It was up tae him tae cut through.

Why else dae the job?

He leant against the railing and sucked in his cheeks. A pucker of his mouth, a swirl of satisfaction and then the release.

He didnae know enough. Could catch in his mind's eye the tail of an idea but it flicked away. Should've stuck in at school. Mostly, it didnae matter, herding lads from workshop tae canteen tae football field. Och aye, he got on fine wi them. He was fit, kept himself in shape, the lads knew that. They knew he wouldnae take any carry-on but would be fair on them. He was damn good at his job. But this boy?

This one would be in and out like a peep of gas.

Setting his shoulder tae the wind he took the path downriver, tugged almost off his feet at the confluence of the Elvern and the Clyde. A gull paddled on an air current before wheeling round wi a mournful screel. Fergus pulled the scarf ower his mouth. He'd make for the park, have another fag, and then get back tae his work.

The wind bowled him intae a shelter, and he sat down,

dimly aware of the whiff of urine. A crisp poke flapped in a wire bin. He fumbled for his pack, lit up and stared out at the broiling Clyde, some hundred yards down the park. The river rumbled past, gulls swinging on the wind, veering west, past Havoc Shore, tae find shelter on the crags. He seldom went back tae that side of town, preferring tae avoid the street where he lived as a boy, where he'd stood wi the neighbours in the road, watching the great cloud of smoke, listening tae the crack of flames, the shouts, the running feet, his heart thumping ten tae the dozen, unable tae move as Paddy Donnelly's house went up in flames.

A boy himself, Fergus couldnae dae anything tae help.

He was only twelve for Christ sake. Only a fuckin wean.

But he hadnae even crossed the street. Stayed nice and safe where he was, out of harm's way. His dad had fought tae get intae the house, but it was awready a tinderbox. In the morning, Fergus got out of his tumbled bed and peered at the scorched windows. Nothing anybody could've done.

He shuddered and took in a cold gulp of air, down tae his stomach.

Later came the metal shutters that made the house look like a grinning monster and didnae hide the licks of soot around the windows. It stayed like that for months, long after they took three coffins down the road, ower the bridge, and through the high street tae the church, the faces of the men like ghouls in their collective grief. Aw Fergus could see, as he stood wi his dad and the other men lining the road, was the look of terror in Paddy's eyes at the window as he mouthed Fergus's name.

And him stuck tae the tarmac, no able tae move a muscle.

Since then he'd seen some sights in Egypt during the war, men cut in half by explosions, but somehow the pale oval of his pal's face was worse.

He flicked away the column of ash on his fag, sucked in a draw, frowned at the burning tip, and deadened it between thumb and finger. He heard Dolly again. 'No like you … tae be acting like a big feartie.' Fluid rushed tae his throat, his nose, his eyes, filling his head tae busting. He rubbed his temples and kicked the bin. The crisp poke took flight.

The boy hadnae even been proven guilty. Least, he was too young tae hang. But maybe he deserved the rope.

Maybe it was too good for him.

Fergus squeezed his eyes shut but imprinted on his mind was a picture of the boy's white fingers poking a petrol rag through a tenement letterbox, setting it alight at one end, a bitter, twisted purpose searing his face. He must've known fine and well two wee lassies would burn tae death. Fergus took the boy by his scrawny neck, encased the cords and bumps, nails gouging soft flesh and pushed him against the tiled wall of the close. The boy's face swelled scarlet until the eyelids drooped.

A pulse of rain angled intae the shelter. Fergus wrapped his arms around his shivering body and rocked. Rocked until the whack in his chest eased. He remembered the boy on the first day, his eyes in the light, a teardrop caught mid-lash.

'He's just a fuckin wean.'

Fergus stood up, and wi the wind willing him on, went back tae work.

1964

Tiramisu

Dolly unlocked the borstal kitchen door, hung her coat on the scullery peg, smoothed the papers in her apron pocket and got on wi the stew. She sliced onions and added them tae the pot wi carrot and turnip, left them tae sweat while she slapped a flank of beef ontae the marble slab, inched her knife under the tarp, chopped the flesh intae chunks and rolled them in flour, her palms padded white. She flung the clumps of beef intae the pot wi two pints of stock and left the lot tae simmer on the gas. At half past ten she poured a cup of coffee tae steady her nerves.

Two and a half hours tae go.

She took her usual seat at the front of the empty canteen, plucked oot the envelope, laid it on the table and took a sip of strong, black coffee, a habit handed doon through the generations on her papa's side. He drank it black fae a bone-white cup, fragrance coiling through the air like a ballerina. He'd take the handle between finger and thumb, tilt it tae his lips, moustache dipping behind the rim and, efter a sigh of contentment, tell her stories aboot Italy. Her childish enthusiasm pressed for mair on Grandma Dolores's café in Roma, Grandma's bosom held aloft like a battering ram, black hair rising magically intae its bun. Grandma weaving aroon wrought iron tables wi her silver coffee pot lifted high.

Two hours and twenty minutes tae the interview.

She put doon her cup, unfolded the notice fae *The*

Chronicle.

> *Tenders invited from suitable interested parties for the café at the pavilion in the park. Summer months only: April to September. Apply to Council Chief ... Mr Connor Begg.*

She wis tae attend the cooncil offices at one o'clock. But she didnae want tae run intae a relative of Archie Begg. This fella wis new tae the town, she'd no been able tae get any gab on him. Anyhow, there'd be bigwigs efter the place, unlikely they'd gie it tae a woman. Dolly rubbed at the age spots splashed across her hand. Whit would a suitable party be for such an establishment? Aye, it'd be a young local in a dark suit.

Well, she wouldnae gie up before she started. She wis prepared.

Stock? She knew a man for that.

Furnishings? She knew a man for that.

Help? She'd only trust a woman for that.

Papa had lost his trust. He'd been a vanilla stick in that hospital bed. 'Oh Dolores, never trust in those people. Preten' you one of them, then ...' He sliced his throat wi an imaginary blade.

The pungency of onions drew her tae stir the stew.

Couldnae be a son of Archie Begg, could it? No son of his would be so high-up in the cooncil. Begg standing in the road, the smirk before he spat on Papa's shoes.

When she wis a girl it wis her job tae polish they shoes. A dollop of wax ontae a cloth, rubbed intae leather, circled ower seams and inlets, her wrist aching. Papa picked up each shoe, turned it aroon and aroon. 'Magnifico, Dolores,' he said, placing it on newspaper tae dry, before leaning doon tae where she knelt, his lips soft on her forehead, his moustache prickly. He slipped sideways tae the door, pinched finger and thumb intae his waistcoat pocket and tossed her a silver thruppence. It hung in mid-air, spinning light before her palms slapped thegither.

'Always be catching the rainbow, Dolores.'

Eleven o'clock. Two hours tae go.

When the afternoon shift arrived at twelve, she went tae the toilet, sprayed another layer of lacquer, and turned in the mirror. Her hair wis still black and her figure trim. Aye, she'd dae, except for the crow's feet aroon her eyes and the wee craters on her chin. Normally this didnae bother her but today? Och, it didnae matter. They'd never gie the daughter of an enemy alien a tender for the café, no the one in the park owned by the Cooncil. But even if there wis the smallest chance, she had tae grab it. She'd done her sums. Wi her widow's pension and savings she could afford tae take the risk. Besides, the war wis a long time ago. Twenty years.

Connor Begg. No necessarily a relative of Archie Begg. Anyhow, this man wis the boss, he wouldnae be seeing the likes of her, she'd be interviewed by a lackey. Nae point in getting worked up. She put on her coat and checked her watch.

At quarter tae one she wis alone in the waiting room. A lass, hardly oot of school, skirt above her knees, came in and took her name.

Dolly tried no tae look at the shire insignia on the wall. She knew some said she wisnae a true Scot, even though in her top drawer lay Papa's letters tae Ma, sent fae the Somme, telling how proud he wis tae be fighting wi his pals. She couldnae read the words withoot seeing him being dragged away fae his ain front door intae the polis van, neighbours pelting stones at her ma's windae, shouting, 'Dirty Tally.'

She rummaged in her bag for her compact, slipped it oot and pressed some dark tan on her cheeks. Scots-Italian, Papa said, acid and sassy rolled intae one.

As she clicked her handbag shut, the door opened and she of the chicken thighs said, 'Mrs Deighan. Mr Begg will see you now.'

'No, ah thought he wis the boss.'

'He's the Head of Department but he does actually meet with … townspeople.'

The girl sniggered. Any of her boys tried that, their ears would smart for a week, but Dolly allowed a lifted eyebrow tae dae its work. The bizzum had the sense tae step back, clattering intae the bin behind her.

Dolly stepped intae a large office dominated by a mahogany, leather topped desk.

A brass clock on the wall chimed one o'clock.

When she recognised the man behind the desk she stalled. A relative for sure.

'Mrs Deighan?' He got up, extended his hand. A young fella, maybe late twenties, guid head of sandy hair. Soft, a pencil pusher. She stared at the hand. 'Pleased to meet you,' he said, taking it back, patting his pocket as though suddenly looking for something.

'Right,' wis aw she could manage.

Papa's protests. *'You make mistake, I no a Mussolini man. I a Scot now.'* Ma gripping him by the shirtsleeve, Dolly held back by her pregnancy, two toddlers at her skirts.

Sandy-hair sat doon, nearly missed the chair. 'Please sit down. I'm Connor Begg.' He scratched his heid, placed his palm on his tie, though it wis awready straight as a plank: green tartan, white shirt, clean collar, married.

She pursed her lips. Might be a son. Maybe jist *il nipote,* a nephew.

He cleared his throat. 'Your tender, Mrs Deighan?'

She closed her eyes. Archie Begg grinning at the scene in the street: the man wi a grudge, the man her father had sacked the year before. He never had time for wastrels as a gaffer.

Might as well be sure. She cut across sandy-hair's mumbles. 'Yer da wouldnae be Archie Begg who worked as a welder at the shipyard, oh, jist before the war?'

His face darkened. 'I believe he did work there in the thirties. A lot of folk from around here worked there then.'

'Uh-huh.'

'Did you know my father, Mrs Deighan?'

'Ma father knew him.'

'And your father is …?'

'Dead. Gabriele Lombardi.'

'I don't recall …'

The clock ticked half a lifetime away.

'Are you alright, Mrs Deighan?'

'Ma papa wis never the same efter a year detained in Barlinnie Gaol. An enemy alien.' The pressure of the day rose in her chest and threatened tae bubble ower.

'That's terrible, I'm so sorry.'

'He said he wis lucky no tae have been sent on the Arandora Star.'

'Oh yes, all those Italian men killed.'

She moved forward, her chest skimming the desk. 'Scots, Welsh, English Italians. Many lived in Britain aw their adult lives. Some had sons who were fightin the Germans. Ma father fought for Britain in the great war.'

'Of course, I didn't mean …' His face wis the colour of cherryade. He fiddled wi his papers.

The eejit wis confused by her line of talk. She'd set him right. And she wis aboot tae dae jist that, when he moved forward and said, 'I'm very sorry. That was foolish of me.'

He looked at her full square. God, he hadnae a clue. Of course he didnae. A young man. Whit did he remember of war? She wanted tae bolt fae the room.

'War makes enemies. It's hard tae forget,' she said, brought up sharp by her ain words.

Begg looked doon, shuffled his papers, cleared his throat. 'Mrs Deighan, your application for the tearooms at the pavilion …'

'Vandals were egged on by clipes and bagotails.' She couldnae shut up.

He looked a wee bit tapioca aboot the gills. 'I'm sorry if coming here has upset you …'

'Ah'm no upset, Son.'

'Your application?'

'Ah know, dinnae bother yersel, ye'll have gied it tae someone else. Must be plenty …' She pulled herself oot of the chair.

'The Committee has approved your application,' he said.

'Whit wis that?' She sank back.

'Yes, it's already been approved.'

'But ah thought ah wis here tae be interviewed.'

'No.'

'But there must've been local businessmen …'

He chuckled, swallowed it back double-quick. 'Aye, a few.'

'How come me?'

'You're the most qualified and experienced applicant. Your references are excellent and you're a trained cook. I have to ask you to sign the contract.'

He turned papers aroon and inched them forward wi a pen. She splayed her fingers tae steady them, wrote oot her name, Dolores Lombardi Deighan, and slid the ice white sheets back.

She had tae know. 'Yer Da moved away fae the town efter the war, if ah remember right?' Despite a slight squeak, she managed tae speak civil, as if asking efter an auld acquaintance.

He seemed tae take it as such. 'Aye, we moved to Corby, for work. I came back here after I married.'

'And yer da?'

'Passed away, Mrs Deighan.' He shook his head. 'Mum left him when I was a boy. He had problems … She rarely spoke of him. But in the end, it was the cancer in the lungs that took him.'

Dolly buffed her mother's wedding ring wi her thumb.

He continued, 'She remarried. I didn't get to see him after that.'

Aye, that wis a turn for the best.

He shifted in his seat. 'I didn't get the chance to know him well. There was always something … You said your father knew him, but did you know him, yourself?'

She had her ain café. Bone china teacups, macaroons, tablet, Edinburgh Rock, coffee beans spilling fae hessian sacks, ice cream rippling through stemmed glasses. Oh, the tinkle of the door as clientele arrived, the tinkle of the till as clientele left. Soon she'd be at the counter in her black dress, the one presently in the Co-op windae, serving cones bright wi hundreds-and-thousands.

He wis waiting.

Maybe he had a right tae know. But it wis hard tae live wi hate. Hard tae die wi it. Och, he wis jist a boy asking efter his father. Whit tae say?

Papa answered. 'Dolores, mia bella. You might be half-Scot, but you no a clipe.'

1964

Isa's Pitch

The airmail letter rustled in Isa's pocket. Jean was doing so well in New York. She scolded Isa when she found out about the last pregnancy. And here she was telling her about this new pill that stopped a woman getting pregnant, no matter the time of the month. All you did was swallow a tablet. Isa took the midwife at the clinic aside and showed her the airmail, but she pooh-poohed it, said it was only to be given if a woman's health required it, and as Isa was fit as a bull this wasn't going to be possible.

All morning the boys had hung like rags over the furniture and across the landing. Now one was on his knees under the kitchen table scrambling for his dice, nearly tumbling the pile of Beanos and Dandys she'd laid out for them. Two were having a tournament to decide First Knight, throwing a spear made from a broom out the back door to roars of delight when it stuck in the tiny patch of wet grass. Trouble was they brought back mud every time they retrieved it. Someone would be black-and-blue before the afternoon ended. The noise was reaching pitch level but, thank God, now the smirr had stopped, she could send them outside to play. Isa sighed, eight long weeks of school holidays yet to go.

'Jamie, go get Connor and Liam, and put the shoes on wee Frank. Sam, get the baw fae the hut.'

Within minutes, five boys spilled out the front door screeching for their pals, leaving Isa to take a break at the kitchen table. The house seemed to exhale with their passing. Charlie crawled over to her feet and pulled himself up to her knee, velvet blue eyes begging for a cuddle. She hiked him up to her lap by the oxters and kissed the top of his silken head, lemon verbena tickling her nose. Ben had slept all through the commotion on his back in the pram, his chubby legs bent so that the knees pointed outwards, the soles of his feet pressed together. A bonny bairn, like the rest of them. A mistake, this time, although she'd never part with him.

She got to her feet, swinging Charlie onto her hip, his fingers clasped in her hair, and poured a cup of tea from the dented pot idling on the stove. They sat on the concrete doorstep, he sooking a lolly, she sipping bitter tea, while downhill at Havoc Shore, clouds scudded over the Clyde. The estate perched on the cliffside, and her back windows felt the strain of the wind and water that drenched the town in the harsh winters, but in the summertime the views were resplendent, the skies a constantly moving panoply of light. Isa savoured this moment of peace, before the bairn woke, or two of them came back before the others, one hurt, the other supervising the return of the casualty, the wail a siren screech as the injured party was guided by the elbow up the hill.

The sky lightened as she sat, clouds thinning and patches of blue forming just before the sun slid out and winked at them, picking out the blackcurrant streaks on Charlie's face as he scrunched his eyes against the glare. The grass began to dry, the heat causing mist to rise in a sheet, droplets glistening like a carpet of diamonds. Those steaming nappies could come off the pulley and be hung out, but she'd wait a few minutes as the weather today was full of devilment.

Two still in nappies. She flushed with irritation every time Angus joked he was raising a fitbaw team. He knew how much she wanted a daughter and he was willing to keep going until that happened, but she wasn't willing to risk more pregnancies. She'd followed Doctor Sloan's advice but it hadn't worked. Out popped Ben in full throttle, number seven on Angus' team list. No delicate wee lass to dress up, no pigtails to plait, no dance classes, no companion for her middle years.

That midwife had a cheek. Isa wouldn't be fit as a bull for much longer if this went on. She'd end up like her poor mother, dead at fifty, her heart swollen after fourteen pregnancies, six of them not surviving the birth or the first weeks of life. Isa hugged the little one next to her. She'd birthed eight, the lost one a steel band around her heart to this day. No, she didn't want to end up an old woman before her time, breathless, wrinkled, fussing over false teeth, her calcium reserves all used up. Isa shivered. That awful day at the dentist, Isa let off school so she could offer her mum a guiding arm home after the extractions. The pervasive smell of gas, Mum's ghastly face, her mouth dripping blood. No, enough was enough.

Though how she'd pitch that one to Angus, she didn't know. He followed the priest to the letter. Father Jim, after belching out frankincense and myrrh on the altar, apoplectic on the pulpit about the rise of contraception and the fall of grace. She smiled, he hadn't heard the grunts and fidgeting in the pews on the women's side of the chapel. Isa'd asked her pal, Lizzie, who'd been to university, all about it, and she said The Pill was legal for married women and not to listen to the midwife. Lizzie talked about women's liberation and something called The Second Wave, and gave her a book by Sylvia Plath, but Isa hadn't been able to make head nor tail of that.

She heard the boys before she saw them, but they'd only been gone twenty minutes, and no one was wailing. She perked her ears to a swell of excited chatter interrupted by a whistle's peep, picked up Charlie and hurried to the front gate. They were piling up the brae, her own five with seven or more of the others, enough for six-a-side and a ref who was giving it laldy on his whistle, while two headed the baw back and forth as they went.

Jamie ran on towards her. 'Mam, Mam.'

The boys crowded around, Connor squeezing through to stand on the bar and swing the gate, eyes stuck on Isa's face.

The bigger boys wore an expression of disgusted disbelief. The last time Isa saw that on her oldest son's face was when Charlie's nappy leaked over Jamie's Celtic strip while they played keepie-uppie, the bairn balanced on the soles of his big brother's feet. The excitement had caused a blast of excrement that would fill a cowshed.

'They've shut the pitch doon.'

This echoed through the crowd, repeated by every boy in turn.

'Aye, closed big gates.'

'Big sign up.'

'We couldnae get in.'

'Aye, they've shut us oot.'

Shut us oot was wailed forth like the chorus of a choir, but these were no choirboys. Jamie's hair aye stuck up like straw, no matter how many combs she broke on it. Her Jamie was the grubbiest boy on the estate, his knees aye scraped and bleeding – he could trip over a ten-ton boulder he could – and wee Frank couldn't keep that tongue behind his lips, it hung out like a spaniel's. The other boys were a ragtag bag of soiled arms, legs and mugs, those mugs silent now, registering their collective outrage, waiting for her response, the only sound the regular squeak of the gate's hinges.

'What does the sign say?'

They all looked to Jamie as the eldest. He screwed up his forehead, the effort of recollection a sore test. He spelt it out.'Football-prohibited-by-order-of-the-council. Any-infraction-will-be-subject-to-a-fine-of-fifty-pounds.'

Isa nodded. 'The Council, eh?'

'Aye, Isa,' the boys chimed. She threw her sons a warning look.

'*Mam,* we mean. Sorry, Mam,' they stuttered.

The pitch was situated at the bottom of the hill, part of the public park. It had been used by the town's boys for as long as she could remember, the grass maintained by the council, and there were two goalposts, one a bit squinty but useful.

'What about the posts?' she said.

'Away,' they howled.

'Good God. But how come there's gates? It's open ground.'

'Wire aw aroon the pitch and gates tied up wi chains.'

This was a problem, especially when you had seven sons. 'Right lads, nothing tae be done the now, leave it wi me. Jist play in the street, and mind the windaes.'

What was the council up to? This was a local amenity. She'd go see Brendan Sweeney, the local councillor, knock on his door, whether he liked it or not. She surveyed the sky, stuck out her palm, the air was drying nicely. She'd hang those nappies out first.

With the nappies billowing on the line, and the crowd fed a stack of jam pieces, the older ones lining up to play penalties in the street, Isa lay Ben in the pram and stuck Charlie on the front seat, his feet soon kicking against her tummy as the pram sprung along the pavement.

Sweeney was a bampot. He'd been a union man till he smelt the decay of the Yards and jumped on the Labour ticket. He wasn't to be trusted, partial to sweeteners and backhanders, but Isa needed to gauge for herself what was going on. Funny how there'd been no notice in the local paper or in the local gossip. She paced downhill to the pitch. It was a flat piece of ground on the periphery of the park, railings erected the full length and breadth of the field with nasty barbed wire strung on top. A set of padlocked metal gates sported a large white sign. She grabbed the cold steel chained around the lock and rattled the gates. Fifty pounds indeed.

She doubled back to Sweeney's house, parked the bairns at the gate, picked her way up the neglected path between banks of nettles, watching out for her nylons, and chapped.

Sweeney peeked around the door with a charmless smile. He smelled like the distillery.

'Oh, it's Mrs McMenamin.' He didn't look surprised. Word travelled fast.

'Brendan.' Isa looked down at his tiny feet.

He shifted back a spot. 'What can I do ye fer?' He chuckled at his wit.

'The fitbaw pitch?'

'Aye, The Council need the land.' He switched his eyes left, over her shoulder.

'Uh-huh.' Isa captured his gaze, brought it back centre.

'It's fer housing, we badly need housing.'

'Uh-huh.'

'Nothing tae be done. It's sorted.' He puffed out his tin man chest.

'I never heard of any notices.'

'It's on record.'

'Where?'

'Well, will be, Monday night, council meeting.'

The bastard squirmed from foot to foot now. He wasn't even a good liar.

'No decided then?'

'Well …'

'A bit premature, that.' Isa threw Sweeney her most withering look, one that Angus said shrank his goolies, turned, charged down the path, kicked off the brake and left the eejit to jangle.

Monday ran her ragged. Her nerves threatened to unstitch her, lay bare her anger and sense of injustice. The washing line snapped with the weight of nappies and she had to wash them again. Surely the council couldn't build on the pitch? The temptation was clear, flat land was at a premium, the town wedged between the Clyde and the hills. But also at a premium were football pitches for the weans.

The meeting was at seven thirty and when Angus came in at six she handed him her pinny which he held at arm's length in bemusement. She changed and left to his protests: 'It'll dae nae guid anyway.' Such was the apathy she'd met all along the street and through the neighbourhood. *Och, ye cannae change these things: better look tae yer back if yer crossin Sweeney.* But they signed her petition good naturedly enough even if they saw it as foolhardy.

The municipal building sat in colourful gardens, and was built from red sandstone, with Alexander Robb, the town's shipbuilding magnate, positioned centre-stage on a high plinth. Isa had only been there once, around the back where the blue lamp marked the police station, on that occasion to collect one very drunk Angus after a night out. She took a deep breath, smoothed down her summer dress and entered by the double doors into a reception area where a clerk stood behind a high desk.

'I'm here for the council meeting.' Her voice pinged off the walls.

The round faced, greasy haired clerk looked up, his eyes asquint. 'You're not Press, are you?'

'Dae I look like Press?'

'Ye never know these days.'

'I'm here as a member of the public.'

He waved towards another set of double doors. 'Sit in the back row. Don't interrupt proceedings.'

Isa tapped her lips with her forefinger and winked at him, gratified when he fell back on his swivel seat.

The chamber wasn't as grand as she'd expected, men in suits sitting around an old scratched table that might have been good in its time but was badly in need of a polish.

Smoke hung between shiny bald pates and sulphurous pendant lights. The odour of dust and old suits hung too long in fusty wardrobes made her sneeze. She stifled a giggle, must've been nerves, although funny enough she didn't feel nervous at all, now she was here. If an argy-bargy was called for she was up for it. She realised she'd giggled again when heads switched in her direction, only to turn away unimpressed. On the back row a young man, in checked shirt and slacks, stood, nodded and invited her to sit near him. He looked familiar and when he took up a notepad and pencil Isa remembered his photo in the Chronicle.

'McCann, Press,' he said, proffering a hand.

'McMenamin. Member of the Public,' Isa returned, smiling broadly.

'Touché,' he said. 'You have a special interest in tonight's proceedings?'

'I dae.'

'Interesting.'

'Why?'

'First time I've had any company here.'

'Ye know the ropes then?'

'Sure. There's something you want to pitch to the council?'

Isa laughed. 'Aye, ye could say that.'

A gavel banged.

The meeting went on … and it went on, etcetera, etcetera, this application and that discussed, agreed, refused, mumbled over, dissected, dismissed. Then it came. Item 41. Planning application for privately built housing adjacent to the Municipal Park. Mumbles of *straightforward enough, unused land,* some shaking of heads, some patting of backs.

The greasy clerk asked, 'Any objections?'

Isa sprung up. 'I object,' she called out in her most authoritative voice, the one that got the boys in line.

What a bustle, what a furore, the newspaperman dropped

his notebook and his pencil rolled away under the rows in front, the councillors' mutters reached a crescendo. Sweeney stood waving his arms in righteous indignation, on his mug an expression of ... aye, it was disgusted disbelief, as though something had shit on him.

The clerk banged his gavel. 'Silence please. We must hear the lady.'

Isa looked sideways to McCann. He gesticulated her forward and she strode up to the table. Grunts, throat-clearing, bad tempers, fidgeting, red faces, messed-up papers, stamping of boots. My, these were just grown boys, she knew about boys, no matter their age. They hated being cooped up, they wanted to get out of here, to the pub, or home to their wives to be pampered and told how special they were. Isa pinned each grumpy face in turn, until the sounds abated and they sat perfectly still, in order.

The chairman cleared his throat.

'On what grounds do you object, my dear lady, er, Miss, Mrs ...?'

'Mrs McMenamin.'

'You have the floor.'

Isa raised herself up and began her prepared spiel: 'I object on the grounds that this land is for the amenity of the townspeople, gifted by the Robb family who founded the shipyards, and is appropriately used by the neighbourhood children as a football pitch which keeps said children out of trouble, suitably exercised, biddable at home and school. The said site has been vandalised by the proposed building company whom I'm sure have misused this guid council's name by fencing it off and threatening children wi fines if they trespass. I have here a petition signed by two hundred and twenty-four of my neighbours, your voters, protesting this development, and I have here a lawyer's letter' — Isa waved her gas bill hoping no one would notice — 'proposing court action if said grounds are no returned forthwith tae their former usage.'

Mouths hung open, one or two palms were pressed to chests, and the gavel hung aimlessly over the table.

Then came a stuttering whine. It was Sweeney. 'But, Mr Chairman, housing is badly needed. These will provide homes for …'

'Four bungalows for private sale,' the chairman said, his finger tracing a line on the open page in front of him.

'What?' said the councillor to his left.

'But it's just a piece of wasteland at the minute,' said Sweeney.

'Mrs McMenamin has just described how well it's used,' the chairman said.

Isa watched closely. Politics in action looked a lot like boys squabbling in the street.

There was jostling going on here, and there were allegiances that didn't seem to include Brendan Sweeney. He was in a wee gang of his own.

A vote was taken. Planning Permission Denied.

Isa stuffed her gas bill back in her pocket and glided around the table to proffer her thanks to the chairman. Oh, how they all hurriedly stood, each face glued to hers, eager for praise. What good boys they were. She didn't disappoint, gave each a warm smile. The newspaper man sat nonchalantly, feet on the back of a chair, pencil in his ear. He gave her the thumbs up. Sweeney hung back, a nasty grimace on his mug.

He'd have to be dealt with at some point. At some point after her appointment the next day, at some point after she'd kicked pregnancy number nine out of the ball park.

1964

Lang Craigs

Boredom had muffled Conall's brain but a sharp pain at the side of his head started him up. The teacher's rheumy eyes pulsed indignation; his fingers pried at Conall's ear. Conall caught at Fife's forearm and twisted. The teacher cried out and let go. Pupil and teacher faced off. Conall burst first and lunged out of his chair into the aisle. Fife bowled backwards. Conall stomped to the door, turned the rickety knob, and glanced back. Fife was on his backside, his hands scrambling for purchase between the desks, the other boys riveted to the scene. Conall sighed and was turning to offer a hand when Fife squeaked, one puny fist stabbing the air, 'Nae mair last chances this time, you waster you. It'll be the gaol next.'

Conall pulled open the door, swung down the corridor, turned left, and shoved open the double doors that led to Cloaks. He wasn't going to leave his duffel coat, not on a day like this. Nor the scarf, hat and sheepskin gloves Eileen gave him last Christmas. But he'd have to hurry. Head would be in the picture soon enough and that he could do without. Bear Brownlie reminded Conall of the bears in Eileen's nature magazines, with his outsize head, black eyes and squashed rugby nose. They'd spatted already and Conall would gladly avoid another round. Bear always won.

His last lecture ran like a waterfall of woe.

'McLaughlin. What have you to say for yourself this time?' The voice boomeranged around the study.

'Ah don't see why ah need tae know about the Kings of England. Ah'm no planning tae live there anytime soon.'

'You aren't?'

'Naw.' Conall peeked up. The face was truly bear-like. Small eyes, square nose, shade and plane. The voice had quietened, the way you detected thunder passing, but something resembling a smile quivered on Bear's lips. Conall was encouraged to try his hand. 'Ah don't need tae know history tae work in the Yards.' That was an undeniable truth. Conall smiled and slouched back in his seat.

'Is that the height of your ambition?' A fist rose and thumped the desk.

Conall flinched but wasn't going to be bullied. 'That's where the work is aroon here.'

'Maybe not for long.' Bear drummed sausage fingers on the desk.

'How come?' Conall didn't believe this ruse.

'There's talk of more closures.' The Head seemed serious enough.

'Ah'll get another job. Ye cannae stop me leaving in eight months.'

Bear clasped his huge hands and leaned over the desk, bringing with him thick odours of tweed and leather. 'Education is your key to freedom. Och, you're wasting your talents, Conall.' Bear sat back and sighed. 'Though, I take your point about English history.' He pulled himself up, lumbered to the shelves under the poky window and picked out a book.

'Here you go, lad.' He handed a heavy tome to Conall. 'See what you make of this. Write two thousand words along the lines of Emigration and the Scots Nation. How about that, eh?'

Conall had taken a whole week to plough through those five hundred pages.

Huffing, he located his peg, took down his coat, pulled

his scarf from a pocket and wound the soft lambswool around his neck. It was as fine a piece of clothing as he'd ever owned. Not likely to have anything like it again. This time Fife was right. He'd be charged with assault, expelled and end up in Approved School. Not gaol, Fife had that wrong. Conall wasn't auld enough for that.

Last chances. As if he gave a bugger. Everyone threw that in your face, your last chance to stay anywhere. Three residential homes flashed past like window displays in a furniture shop, three schools less clearly defined, with their Fifes, their own brand of grizzly Heads, and Shakespeare. Aye, next time he went fishing he'd spout out to the reeds, *To be, or not to be, that is the question: Whether 'tis nobler in the mind to suffer the slings and arrows of outrageous fortune, or to take arms against a sea of troubles ...* load of shite. He fastened the toggles of his duffel coat and put on a glove.

Not one of them listened to him. Best to leave them all behind, get his stuff and make his own way. Sure, he could fish and trap by himself. His grandfather had taught him all he needed to know to survive. He'd got on fine before Eileen turned up.

Heavy footsteps approached from far down the corridor. Conall stuck on the other glove, grabbed his satchel and shot out through the side door into the yard. He was exiting by the gate when Bear bawled, 'McLaughlin get back here right now ...' Conall didn't tarry. He bowled around the corridor and flew down the lane, skidding onto his hip on gravel, then up like lightning, and onto the main road heading for Eileen's before she got home from the shops.

Breathing heavily, Conall slowed as he took the brae to the terraced council house. The street was empty, as expected at two o'clock on a weekday in October. He glanced downhill at Havoc Shore, at the sheet of steel that was the Clyde, at the path where Eileen liked to walk Sprinter every morning, rain, hail or snow. The moans of low flying seagulls drifted upwards as he bit off a glove, caught it under his other arm, and fingered the key in his pocket. He'd never been trusted with a house key before, but Eileen had insisted on it the day he arrived. 'So ye can feel free tae come and go and no have tae worry about me being home. Ah don't want ye tae be locked out in the cold.' She meant she trusted him not to steal anything. And she could trust him. Conall was no thief.

He let himself in by the back door to Sprinter's whines. He could hardly push the door open for the dog's weight. He'd be thinking it was walkie time. One honey-brown eye came into view. 'Back boy, there ye go.'

The retriever slithered back on his rump, his tongue hanging loose in a doggy smile. Conall snapped shut the door, dropped his bag, and bent down to fondle the silken chest. Something caught in his throat, and he swallowed it back, setting his mind against affection for this animal. The dog would be alright; he'd been here long before Conall, and Eileen adored him.

The kitchen smelt of freshly baked bread and Conall's nose led him to two floured loaves on Eileen's wooden board. They were warm to the touch and his mouth watered. He looked down at Sprinter whose eyes stuck fast to the bread. Eileen wouldn't mind if Conall took a slice, especially when this would be his last, unless he took a few more for his lunch and tea, maybe with some cheese and her grand ham. Just until he could find his own sustenance. A bit of butter too and maybe he'd fill a wee jar with her raspberry jam. He fetched the bread knife from the drawer and cut into the loaf, lifted the lid from the butter dish and slapped an inch on the slice, beating and spreading until it stuck. The dog's saliva dripped on the linoleum. Conall shook his head, tore off a corner of bread and pitched it to the animal who caught it between the jaws, dropped it, licked off the fat, and sat down to gnaw at the crust. Conall would miss Eileen's food, she made everything from scratch: big roasts, soups thick with ham and turnip, apple pies freshly baked on a Saturday morning, the crust where the juice had browned begging to be broken off. She was also a dab hand at Pontoon, and she could beat any man at table tennis down at the Labour Club. Seemed to Conall, Eileen knew everyone in the town and was related to half of them.

He'd best get on. She'd be home soon, and what could he say? 'Ah'm home early because ah floored the teacher. Thanks for everything, ah'm off.' He clapped the dog who looked up from his prize and gave him a quizzical look but wasn't curious enough to rise. Conall raced upstairs, still chewing the last of his bread, looked out some clothes and shoved them into his rucksack. He picked up his binoculars from the shelf, took his knife from the drawer, found his fishing trousers in the airing cupboard and changed out of his uniform and shoes into heavy corduroys and boots. He got his sleeping bag from the top of the wardrobe. His fishing gear was in the hut, he'd take that as he left.

Back in the kitchen, Sprinter sat expectantly in his basket. Conall felt the dog's eyes follow him as he fetched food items from the larder, filled a flask with tea, and took another down from the shelf to fill with water from the tap. He had a fair load now, but he was strong. Eileen's jotter, where she noted her shopping, lay on the counter at the back door. Maybe he should write a note. No, he'd lock the door and leave the key under the mat. It'd take her a while to find it but then she'd know he wasn't coming back. He patted Sprinter one last time and the dog lay down whining in his basket.

Conall strode away from the river, across the housing scheme, towards town, keeping to back streets just in case the School Board was nosing about. He eyed the hills ahead. A low mist covered the line where the crags met the sky, a blending of hill and heaven. He crossed the back road, quiet at this time of day, and swung over the low stone wall into deep vegetation: brambles, heather and furze. It sprang under his boots as he tramped through and he had to take care of his eyes on low branches and thorn. He drank in the taste and smell of sap and soil, damp and thick. Although this place offered shelter from the cold it was too close to the town to be a sanctuary and he pushed on to the clearance of fields. Fields that were draped over the hills, fields only fit for hardy sheep, fields that were open to any prying eye. Not that he'd be missed yet. Bear would believe him to be at home, and Eileen would believe him to be at school. Conall stopped. Och, the eaten loaf. He couldn't pin that one on Sprinter. That would lead her to his room, the missing stuff and, Eileen being Eileen, she'd look under the mat for the key. She'd be down at the school by now nagging the face off Brownlie. He bit his lip. Eileen always had a kind word and a gentle touch. She darned his socks and cut his hair when it lopped over his forehead. It was Eileen who took him to the dentist to get that tooth out two summers past, not long after he arrived. The only person who'd ever told him she loved him. He thought he'd misheard that. In trouble again, note home from Bear, the look of confusion on her flour-streaked face as she read it. His sorry explanation. And then, her fine sky-blue eyes filling. 'Ye know ah love ye sorely, Conall McLaughlin, but ye sure dae try a body's soul.'

Conall shook off the memory and pulled himself up the steep hillside, making for the woods of Ardeer estate. He could have taken the road, but he might've been spotted there. For sure, one of Eileen's relatives would just happen to be up at the auld mansion house, now a hospital where babies were born, on one errand or another and would they nod and pass? Och no. It'd be, 'Conall, does Eileen know ye're off the school?' He'd be manhandled back down the road in front of the whole town.

He climbed over a stile and into covered terrain where

he was less exposed, lay down his gear and sat on a rock. His nose and chin were numb with cold and he'd have to get going if he was to make the hideout by dark. He glanced at the sky; night would fall in a couple of hours. But least it was dry, he'd be able to get a fire going. Grandpa had taken him many times to their hideaway beside the stream. You went far into the woodland to find it and it was well camouflaged by tree and bush. Many a night they'd sat out under the stars – mainly in the summer months now Conall thought about it – and he'd listen to Grandpa's tales of the injustices done to their forebears. The clearances of men and their families off the land enraged Grandpa, whose own kin had walked all the way from Oban after being thrown out. Conall had read more about that in Bear's book, further proof that you didn't need education to be wise about the world. Grandpa had known everything about life and Conall didn't need no schooling.

He picked up a stone and fired it into a tree. A wood pigeon slewed off. All that was before Grandpa's heart attack, before Conall went to that rubbish children's home. Conall believed himself to be alone in the world and had run off, but they always caught him, until Eileen turned up waving away the woe-betide-you reluctance of Matron.

Conall got up and tramped on. Matron was right, he only brought trouble. The air smelled of mulch and leaf, of winter heather and was so sharp it could bleed your tongue. Soon he was nearing the edge of his deep wood. Downhill, the Clyde stretched through the basin; a grey cargo ship sailed towards the estuary. He left that sight behind and pushed towards the trees, relieved now that he was far away from people and closer to his ideal companions, the great raptors of the sky. What a life it would be to soar over the hills, to swoop on prey, to be part of mountain, river and sea. No more essays, no more four walls, no more, 'Buck up, Conall McLaughlin.'

No more rules.

Jeez, how that Eileen nagged. Shoes to be polished just so – he even had to make his own bed the way she liked it. And change it every week. Grandpa had never changed the sheets on the bed unless they were dirty through some spillage or other. He said, 'Wimen, they'll tie ye tae their apron strings.' Said it with a glint in his eye that Conall couldn't read.

The ground was uneven, but Conall's boots were heavy soled, and he took satisfaction from the strength in his thighs and the regular pulse of his heart. He'd almost reached his destination when he stumbled, his attention taken by a pitiful whine to the west just at the foot of Lang Craigs. It came again. An animal in pain was not something Conall could ignore. On the other hand, a wounded animal, out here on the hill, might be a dangerous prospect. He listened closely for another sound, and it came with force, as though the creature sensed his presence. Conall turned, reluctance overtaken by curiosity. He shrugged off his rucksack and let it slip down his body, ditched his fishing rod and stepped forward with purpose, following the whines, and sounds of scratching. Claws, hoofs? He climbed a small brae, and, on the rift, a black-and-white spaniel lay on its side, trying to rise but failing every time. A broken leg? Or a thorn in a paw, or maybe he'd been shot. Sometimes trappers up here hunted rabbits. The dog's eyes rolled back as he sensed Conall near him. Its whines accelerated.

Conall approached the animal eye to eye making sure there was no threat as, step by step, he came closer. Its fur lay matted across its rump and there was only pleading in the dark brown eyes, the whites glowing in the black face. The dog stopped whining and now his breath rose and fell in rapid, short gasps. Conall hunkered down, whispering as he flopped his hand, palm inwards, towards the dog's snout. It tried to lift its head, but the tail rose and thudded back in permission. Conall fell to his knees and looked over the animal, spotting a swelling on the hindleg, before giving him a reassuring pat on the neck. 'Well, chappie, looks like ye might've broken a leg there, but here's hoping it's only a sprain.'

The matting proved to be dirt, there was no cut on the skin, but the dog wouldn't be able to walk. Conall needed to go for help; that meant going back into town. There wasn't a farmhouse nearby and this didn't look like a working dog. Although he had no collar, he looked like a house pet. Well fed, keen, friendly and intelligent, he'd been well cared for. Maybe got lost chasing rabbits or some such. Damn it. Conall scratched his head, stood up and peered about. The dark was rolling in across the sky. He'd have to get the animal off the hill by himself. Take him to the vet's in Church Street. Though he may have closed by the time they got there. Maybe take him to Eileen first. Conall looked down at the spaniel. Damn stupid place to end up with a broken leg. Hadn't he a nice warm fireplace to sit at, and a bowl of beef and dripping to lap up? Silly creature out on the hills alone this time of year. Whatever the dog saw in Conall's eyes made it give a shrill bark. It sounded uncannily like a command.

'Hey, now, ye're no the boss here. Ah'll no leave ye, don't worry, but ye surely dae try a man's soul.'

Conall bit back his frustration and dug in his pocket for his penknife. His fingers touched cool metal and he drew out the house key. Damn it. He dropped it back in and fumbled further for the knife and made strips of his good scarf.

Eileen would understand.

The dog didn't protest when Conall wrapped the leg, layering the scarf like a bandage wound from top to bottom and tucked in against the ankle. He poured some water from his flask over the dog's mouth and it licked with gusto. Conall hid the fishing rod under a bush, retrieved his rucksack, balanced it on one shoulder, then lifted the whimpering dog up on his opposite hip. Och, there was nothing to him at all, light as a whisper. Conall turned around and made for the road, just in case a relative of Eileen's might pass and offer him a hand.

1971

Nae Bevvy

Mary McCloud blustered out of the office door, black raincoat billowing around her ample hips as the wind whistling up the dank stairwell caught her.

Isa wished it would sweep Mary up and fling her in the Elvern.

The woman was a nosy so-and-so, a gossip with no restraints, here to complain about her neighbour yet again, Mary was one of the town's obnoxious crows that huddled in packs, pecking at promising crumbs left by innocent passers-by. Or worse, dropped shells on the roads for trucks to shatter. That was Mary's intention this Friday evening. To lever Isa into a position of dropping her might on the poor neighbour to have her evicted. And for what?

Because of a nasty fight between two drunk husbands two decades ago, in the fifties, that had been kept on the simmer by the McClouds.

Isa had given her short thrift. 'Mrs McCloud, if ye've a complaint about your neighbour take it up wi the housing officer.'

'Ah'm taking it up wi you.' Mary clung to her oversize shopper and stuck her chin out over her chest, beady black eyes darting left and right.

'I cannae help ye. I don't have the authority. Proper channels are …'

'That woman's keeping a filthy hoose.' Two coal eyes

blasted ire.

'I've no say wi the housing office.'

Mrs McCloud hadn't believed that, but her distrust of authority kept her temper at the back of her tongue.

Isa wondered why she continued to play referee between constituents who wanted to tear out each other's throats. Why she continued to listen to dire stories of illness, poor housing, unemployment, bad landlords, and debt collectors. All the detritus of a town groaning under the weight of poverty, and now looming mass unemployment.

She wasn't even paid for it. And now as a widow, with a piddling pension and relying on welfare herself, she could do with a proper job. Seven boys to feed and clothe, Mary McCloud was the least of her worries.

Isa rose and stepped to the window. She rubbed a space clear in the condensation and peered out. Mary was indeed struggling to keep her feet as she traipsed along the Elvern's path. A sudden wave of river water flooded the quay and slapped Mary full tilt so that she lost her footing.

Isa bolted for the door, grabbed her coat, and rushed downstairs to the close mouth. She was halfway down the street when a tall figure grabbed Mary by the arm, hoicked her to her feet and dragged her away from the river to the bus stop.

Shaking her head, Isa turned back to the close and climbed upstairs to the dingy one-room office, feet squelching in her pumps, the back of her nylons soaked.

Her office was a single-end on the first floor of Leckie's building, another rat-infested disgrace of housing, smelling of damp and rotting plaster, used for the unfortunates who couldn't get on Havoc Council's housing list. Either because they didn't know how, or because they didn't know someone with clout.

Isa hung her raincoat on the hook behind the door, ignoring the high pitched argie-bargie from an upstairs flat, and ran her fingers through her wet hair, shaking off a shower of raindrops. Surgery evening hadn't been busy because of the weather, yet another summer's day spoiled by heavy rain.

After setting the teapot on the rickety stove, she sat down, opened her fag packet, and tapped out a cigarette. This would have to stop. She couldn't afford to smoke. The cigarette slotted back in the pack, she wondered what had happened to all her plans and dreams. How wet behind the ears she had been, thinking she could make a difference. To her annoyance, her eyes filled with tears. Maybe she should shut up shop for the night. No, she couldn't, one more constituent to see.

Rain battering the window, wind howling through the gaps in the door, she let her mind wander back to that day when the idea of being a town councillor had been put to her. A stab of guilt pierced her; Angus's second anniversary just past, and she was resurrecting old fancies. But it always comforted her to remember. Like a cosy blanket on this damp night, it was a harmless indulgence.

Seven years ago, not long after her first appearance at a council committee as a member of the public with a petition, she had reason to file a death notice on behalf of her auld neighbour. Mrs Doyle's man had passed in his sleep and she'd come to Isa for help.

Isa had wheeled baby Ben in his pram to the Chronicle's offices in the High Street. After parking the pram at the door, she went in to find the desk unmanned. She pressed the bell, there was no response. Anxious that the bairn would begin complaining, she pressed several times more, making a right racket, but still no one attended. Swearing under her breath, she raised the counter flap and went through to a short corridor, where the tap-tap of a typewriter drew her to a frosted glass door. She pushed it open and there was the newspaper fella, Grant McCann, who had egged her on at the council meeting.

He looked up, startled, and then a broad smile stretched from ear to ear. 'Why, it's Mrs McMenamin, saviour of the football pitch. Here to cause more trouble?' He laughed.

She bristled. 'Indeed not, I'm here tae file a death notice and there's no a soul at the counter. You must lose a lot of business.' She pursed her lips, agitated now by his joviality.

He shook his head as if his theory were proven.

Cheek.

Worse, he approached and slid past her, causing her to breathe in mightily. She turned and followed him to the reception. He opened the flap and gestured her through. She had to skim past him and was forced to meet his twinkling brown eyes, eyes that suited his sandy hair, eyes that brimmed with knowledge and experience, though he was younger than her. She noticed the rough of his beard, the short hairs shadowing his jaw, the arc of his top lip.

He took the details and the shillings. 'Be in the paper on Thursday. By the way, you're a natural. There's a by-election coming up. Be good to see a woman on this old man's council.'

She huffed and took her change.

But the idea had taken hold and here she was.

Aye, Grant was a handsome man, and the thrill of attraction had stayed with her all these years, but they'd done nothing about it. She'd been a married woman and now, as a widow with seven children, it was unseemly.

The teapot lid spewed steam; Isa rose and turned off the gas. She lifted the pot at the handle with a dishcloth and poured a steaming dark cup of tea, adding some lukewarm milk from a bottle kept on the windowsill.

She sat down on her chair at the side of the table. Not behind it, that was for doctors, priests, lawyers, headteachers, those in her life who were bent on intimidation. She looked at her list. Just one more tonight. Big Matt McLean. It wasn't like Matt to be seeing his local councillor; that would mean twenty minutes absence from his seat in the Cutty Sark. He'd be half-cut by now. Matt was more of a hands-on kind of problem solver, punching a problem into touch. Things must be bad to bring him to her door. Of course, the yards were in trouble, which meant they were all in trouble. Sold down the Clyde by Westminster. He'd be worried about redundancy, though there would be worse off than him, men with families. Thousands of them. More when you consider the businesses feeding from the Yards. But Matt's wee brother would still have work at the butcher's, and Matt was nothing if not resourceful.

She caught the sound of him before he appeared. A whistling tune under the howl of the wind. The stamp of boots, and the door burst open in a frenzy of man and the elements. On his tod, no Billy in tow. That was a relief. Matt was manageable, Billy was a wrecking ball.

Matt banged the door shut behind him so hard the hinges groaned. He took a step forward, froze, opened his mouth, closed it again, frowned, then, as if it were a mighty insult, grabbed at his cap and twisted it so hard the water drained onto the cracked linoleum, creating a piteous puddle.

'Och, sorry, missus.'

'It's awright, Mister McLean … er … Matt, isn't it?'

'Aye, Mrs McMenamin, Isa?'

'Sit down. Take off yer coat.' Isa gestured to the peg on the door, and a chair.

He hesitated and Isa got up, in part to put him at ease, in part to be closer to his gaze and not feel so diminutive. She noticed he smelt of damp cotton and leather, thankfully not of barley or hops. He was well over six feet tall, rangy, dark haired, and oftentimes glowering. The stringy scar on his left cheek didn't help soften his demeanour, though his eyes were a vivid gentian blue under the shaggy black brows and though wet, his hair was full and wavy, flopping over his forehead with an innocence reminiscent of boyhood. The long sideburns were an attempt at fashion but failed miserably. This man was an enigma in the town; sometimes hard man, would be womaniser, family man to his siblings, a grafter, he had his own set of rules.

They were about the same age, having come up primary school together before secondary separated the boys from the girls. His father had been a drunk who beat his wife. Rumour had it he'd been helped into his coffin by Matt himself, but a blind eye would have been turned. None of Isa's business and she wouldn't have blamed any boy for protecting his mother or sisters if it had come to that. The scar had been a gift from the old sod, so you reap what you sow.

Was she reaping what she'd sown? Sitting here, on a miserable night, alone, with a man like Matt, defenceless.

Anyway, it hadn't been her plan to be in this situation. McCann had started all this.

Matt was still standing, his coat held out in front. Isa took it, hung it up and gestured to the plastic chair. 'Sit down, Matt.'

She wasn't afraid of Matt. His value system may be unique, but no woman would ever be at risk from him. He was more likely to smother her with misplaced intentions.

Matt surveyed the chair, eyes contemptuous of its ability to hold him. He picked it up, rocked it to and fro, frowned, stamped it back on the floor with a bang, and lowered his length onto the seat.

Isa sat down. 'What can I help ye wi?'

'Er …' The blue eyes widened in confusion.

'Matt, it's awright. Jist tell me.'

'Billy, It's oor Billy. Aye.' He slapped his thigh as though he'd got an answer right.

Isa waited, nodding her head in encouragement.

'Wondered if ye could help him get his ain place, being on the council and aw.'

'Has he applied?'

'Naw.'

'He'll need tae put in an application form.'

'In writing?'

'Aye. You could fill it in for him, and he'd only need tae sign it.'

Relief relaxed the man and he smiled. 'He can write his name.'

'Guid. Ye'll need tae get the form from the office in Church Street.'

'The housing office?'

'Aye, the housing office.'

'How long will that aw take?'

'Might be a while. Has Billy any er ... special needs?'

'Aye, he needs a guid slap on a daily basis.'

'No. I mean, any health issues maybe ...'

'Och aye, ye mean his fits and that?'

'He has convulsions?'

'Naw, jist wee bad turns.'

'If the doctor supports his application, he'll move up the list.'

'Nae bother, the doctor's aye saying Billy needs his heid examined,'

'Literally?'

'Whit?'

'Never mind.'

Matt sat on, smiling to himself as though he was recalling a delightful episode of some kind.

'Matt, was there anything else?'

'Aye, aye, I wondered if ye could talk tae Billy for me. He disnae want tae move.'

'But he'd need tae sign, unless ye're evicting him.'

'Naw, I couldnae throw him out.'

'Well, why dae ye want him tae leave?'

Matt looked from side to side and behind him. Dumped

his seat closer and whispered, 'I cannae get a lumber wi him stuck tae my shadow. My plan was this. If I could get him a hoose, a wee flat, say, and make it nice, then I could mibbe persuade him tae try it out, like one night the first week, then two ...'

'I see.' Isa considered this to be a reasonable plan. She could see the dilemma. Being single was no fun. Everyone needed a soulmate, a confidant. Like Grant. They were friends now, that was all. He was a good ally to her in her work, and sometimes he'd turn up unannounced after a meeting or after surgery just for a blether or to walk her home in the dark, though not likely on this bleak, dour night. He never crossed a line. Kidded her about them going away for a dirty weekend, making her blush every time.

She sympathised with Matt's situation. Billy was a huge responsibility. A man who'd never grown up. If Matt could get a bit of space, but still be supportive, that might be a good plan for them both. Isa could help them manoeuvre their way through the red tape. That was within her rules.

'Tell ye what, Matt. The family house is in yer name?'

'Aye.'

'Then ye need tae state clearly tae the council officer that ye're throwing Billy out and he needs another place.'

'Lie, ye mean?'

'It wouldnae be a lie if ye decided it was necessary, even if ye were tae change yer mind at any point.'

Matt nodded sagely. 'I get yer drift. Whit will I tell Billy?'

'Tell him he'll aye have a home wi you, but he's entitled tae his ain place as he's a grown man now.'

'Dae ye think that'll work?'

'So ye'd like me tae speak tae him, put the plan tae him, and ...'

'Och, aye. He'd listen tae you.'

Isa doubted that, but where she saw a need she had to fill it.

She started to rise. 'Bring him tae see me. Another night. We'll sort it out.'

He sat on, staring at the floor. The wind had quietened and now the rain merely pattered the window. In the near quiet she could hear Matt's breath quicken.

'Is there something else, Matt?'

He straightened up, shook his head, and said woefully, 'There's tae be nae bevvying.'

Isa lowered herself back on her seat, and waited, not having a clue what might come next. But she had learned that sometimes the real problem took time to show itself. Matt's countenance had taken on the aspect of deep grief, not surprising when he was discussing threats to his most beloved pastime. She watched the struggle play across his features, strong features, dark, invulnerable except for the bright, crumpled scar.

In a world of his very own now, he uttered, as if in imitation of a higher, more sensible voice, 'Nae hooliganism,' and nodded an apparent acceptance of that idea. 'Nae vandalism,' came next, accompanied by a tilt of the head as if this fact were questionable. Then, he came to. 'Aye, aw that, but why, Isa, why the hell, nae bevvying?'

The man's eyes moistened, his hand shook, and one foot tapped the linoleum in a jig. Isa frowned, she recognised distress when she saw it. Maybe Matt had come to his senses and was thinking of joining AA. This was a human being in a crisis. She had to go lightly here, help him make the right decision.

She woke up from her saintly benevolence when he slapped the table, and the teacup shook out its dregs of tea leaves.

'Ye're well thought of,' he announced, his eyes fastening to hers.

This was a compliment, what she'd become a councillor for, to help her neighbours.

'Matt, the meetings are on a Wednesday night, ah've a leaflet someplace.' She moved to open the desk drawer.

He ignored her. 'It's that shop steward Reid. Jimmy Reid, Govan man. Marvellous fella, but nae bevvy?' He rolled his tongue around as if to spit, thought better of it, and swallowed hard, his Adam's apple hitching at his throat. 'That's for the birds.' Matt tore his eyes away, satisfied he'd landed the point, and looked about him as if there were a spy in the room. Clocking there were no prying eyes, he leaned forward, a hand on each splayed thigh, and announced, 'There's tae be a work-in.'

Clarity shot through. Upper Clyde Shipbuilders were in receivership, the Tories had taken the feet from under the industry, withdrawing support. The towns up and down the Clyde were in shock. The council had been caught on its back legs. Even though Havoc's yard had closed years ago the town depended on the other yards. It was a disaster. Nothing much to be done. But what was that to do with drink?

'The council is discussing what tae dae, how tae assist. We've written tae the government, protested … I can help get ye ontae the dole, a rent holiday maybe.'

'Naw, Hen. I don't need money. I've nae weans and Billy will be working. We're awright. If the yards shut, I'll go wherever the work is, London if need be.' He spat intae a hanky that had crawled out of his shirt pocket. 'Naw, it's the bevvy.'

'Aye?'

'I thought you could speak person tae person wi Jimmy Reid and tell him tae pipe doon on that one. A work-in is fine. I'm up for that, but whit I dae in my ain time is up tae me. As ye know I'm an upstanding citizen, maist of the time, nae vandalism fae me, though I cannae say the same for Billy. But I don't think it's right for me no tae be allowed a hauf through whit could be months.'

'But I've never met Mr Reid.'

'Yer a councillor. Go see him.' He nodded as if the deed was done.

'Tell ye what. I'll jist get on my best coat and hat, board the night train tae London and tell Edward Heath tae bugger off.'

'Who's that then?'

'The Prime Minister.'

'Whit's he tae dae wi it?'

Isa sighed. She had the gist of it now. A work-in. Very novel. Would that work? Good on Jimmy Reid for trying. Of course, best behaviour or the whole plan would topple. She'd heard of Reid. He was a strong shop steward. But was he strong enough to take on the Tories and to keep the yards pulling together?

'When did Mr Reid say aw this?'

'The day. Big meeting.'

Isa knew something had been on the cards but not this. 'I think when Mr Reid says nae bevvying, he means on the job. Dae ye drink at work jist now?'

He looked at Isa as if she'd smacked him across the face. 'Absolutely not. I'm a gaffer, wi responsibilities. Hen, have ye ever been on a ship wi a welder?'

'No …'

'Ye could set yersel and yer mates alight if ye werenae compos mentis.'

'I see. Very guid. Listen, Matt, ye won't be expected tae be at work night and day. There will likely be shifts. As now. Ye'll be free tae dae whatever ye like off the clock as ye are now. As long as ye don't drink yersel stupid and bring the Union intae disrepute.'

'Right.' He slapped his forehead. That must have smarted some. 'Yer a marvel. Ah knew ye'd set me straight. Dae ye think it'll work, this work-in?'

'Well, it's better than a strike, which would play intae the government's hands. They want tae close the yards down.'

'Aye, that's whit Reid said. Thanks Isa.'

He reached over. She leaned back. He grabbed her hand and patted it in his huge mitt like she was a six-year-old.

Isa was recovering her dignity, straightening her cardigan, clearing her throat, when a movement caught her eye. Through the condensation at the window a disembodied head floated. Isa let out a screech. Matt jumped up and turned. 'How the hell? Och, it's Billy. I tellt him tae wait outside. He's climbed up the drainpipe.'

As Billy hovered, Matt turned to Isa, clicked his heels, and with unexpected grace, bowed from the waist. He might have had a rose stem between his teeth it was so well done.

'Ye're a star, Hen.' He pulled a full quarter bottle of Bells from his trouser pocket and stuck it in her face.

'No, ye're awright, Matt. Mind and get those forms now.'

'Whit forms?'

'The housing forms.'

He was throwing on his coat, Billy still wavering at the window, when he let out a riff of short, apologetic coughs followed by, 'Ye wouldnae fancy a trip tae the Palais on Saturday night?'

She darn well did fancy that, but not with Matt. 'I'm a married woman, Matt. Well, widowed.'

'Widowed is awright by me.' He grinned.

Isa shook her head, a half-smile playing on her face. Matt couldn't cope with one boy never mind seven.

'Too bad. Ye're a guid looking woman. Ye must have a load of fellas asking ye out.'

Only one, Isa thought.

Matt winked before manhandling the door and bursting out.

Isa almost winked back.

She heard the curfuffle as he grappled Billy off the windowsill, their voices shrill, followed by their footsteps fading down the street.

Isa gathered her bag and coat and looked around. It wasn't such a bad place; it did the job. And no doubt more would need to be done now this work-in was planned. The workers and their families would need support. Her mind whirred.

She locked the door, ventured out of the close, and pulling on her raincoat, ignored the smell of cooking lard and frying chips. The rain had lightened to a sun-kissed shower, steam was rising from the pavements, she'd be home in no time. Busy thinking about big Matt and the work-in, it took a moment to notice Grant waiting for her on the corner, his sandy hair tousled, the smile she loved playing on his face.

Startled by the quickening of her own heart, she vowed that this time, when he asked her, she'd say yes.

1976

The Thin Place

School holidays are made for drawing, even after nights of chaotic dreams, those chest-tightening searches that make me wake in a lather. But every time I go back to the sketches, I throw down my pencil. Some detail of the parapets is missing, or the scale of the wall is off, or the fatal drop from the balustrade isn't the right height, or how the bridge connects to the big house is wonky. And I'm never sure if I've nailed the number of mismatched windows on the east side or if the turrets are positioned correctly.

'Mum, I'd like to pick some bluebells for Granny's grave.'

'Oh, Gabs, what about our walk to Aunt Isa's with the twins?' She looks up, balancing Theresa on her knees, clutching two ankles in one hand, the other whipping off a caked nappy. Beth's snoring in her cot.

I nip my nose so as not to boak. 'You go on. I'll run up the hill and get some flowers from the bluebell wood. I'll bring some home for you too.'

Mum always moans about me going off alone to Ardeer. Makes an excuse to come with me or find something else for me to do. Least now with the new babies, I'm not the centre of things.

'Alright, Gabs, on you go, but be back for tea before your dad gets home. And mind, don't lose track of yourself, daydreaming again.'

I grab my pad and pencils, fly out the gate, saunter up the street and, when I'm sure no one can see me, spin through the archway to Ardeer Estate. A whole afternoon off, free from walking the twins' squeaking double-hooded pram.

The wide grit path winds into the hill, wildflowers peek from long grass and when I gain higher ground, rhododendrons form a ten-foot guard either side. As the town hushes, footsteps kick up gravel behind me. I turn, pebbles and dirt trickle down the path as if someone had tripped but there's not a soul to be seen. Shaking my head clear, I climb on. A few moments later someone laughs, and I stop, circling round, but the path's deserted. I must've imagined it, or perhaps it was a bird, a herring gull's manic cackle.

I rest on my usual boulder and catch my breath at the chequered quilt expanding before me. Grey roads, leading to the High Street and the Clock Tower, cut orange-roofed housing estates. The Clyde glistens in the sun and I can just make out the silver thread that's the Elvern.

Before she became ill, Granny often took me along the river walk but she never took me up Ardeer as she didn't like crossing the bridge. She always took an interest in my drawings, though.

'Give me that notebook of yours to please my eye, you'll be a fine artist one day.'

'Just like Pops, eh Granny.'

'Such an imagination, Gabrielle. Make sure you do well at school. No more of that staring into outer space with those bonny blue eyes.'

'Can't help it Granny, I get sore bored in the class and now the teachers have stopped me doodling, I have to go inside my own head.'

'I know. Your Pop was the same. A dreamer, born on the wrong planet. Away with the fairies at times.' She chuckled. 'Aye talking to himself and, when I'd tell him to pipe down, he'd say I was disrespecting his ancestors.'

'What ancestors?'

'Never you mind that, just keep at your work.'

To stop my eyes welling up, I strike out the view. I'm engrossed when a cool breeze brushes my neck and I half-turn on my boulder. A boy around my age is standing behind me, hands on hips. Beside him a perky spaniel with long black-and-white ears and a feathered tail stares at me before dipping into the longer grass, nosing the ground. The boy watches me closely. He smiles and my hand trembles, shooting the pencil off at a tangent to land at his feet. Laughing, he bends to pick it up. Mortified, my cheeks burn. They're molten by the time he inches onto my boulder, the warmth of his leg pressing mine. I creep away as much as I can without falling off or risking a sore bum on a crack. The dog returns panting, circles our perch and slumps down on its belly, eyes fixed on the boy's face.

'This is the best seat in Havoc.' The stranger hunkers on his elbows and peers at the view.

'Yes, I sit here often and draw.' Despite my discomfort, I'm determined not to move. The cheek of him, doesn't he realise he can't sit beside someone without permission?

As if he could read my thoughts, he says, 'Of course, this is your seat. I'm just a visitor here.'

When he turns and looks directly at me, I notice the irises in his violet eyes are specked with gold, and his soft blonde hair is a few shades lighter than mine. He picks up my drawing and studies it a moment, a half-smile teasing his lips.

'This is pretty good, you have talent. I'm Ewan and this is Sam.'

'Gabrielle.'

I'm reassured. Daft really, as if knowing a person's name makes them alright. But there's something else licking at the corner of my mind. He reminds me of someone, but I can't place him.

'Are you walking up to the house?' He points to the path. His hands are pale, the nails clear on long, delicate fingers.

'Sure.' Somehow, I don't want him to see me sketching the bridge or the house. 'I was going to pick some flowers. I'll just leave my stuff here.'

Sam gambols ahead in the foliage, his tail peeking in and out of the long grass as we amble up the path.

'Why doesn't Sam wear a collar?' I ask.

'He doesn't need one,' Ewan says.

'What about a lead? What about the roads?'

'He doesn't have a problem with those.' He winks at me.

No one ever winks at me. I cover up my embarrassment with noise. 'Where you from?'

'Only here for a bit. I come from a long way off, over the water.'

'Aye, where's that, then?'

'It's just where my home is.'

Most likely it's across the Clyde at Greenock and he's trying to sound mysterious.

We make a good pace, my legs stretching to keep up. He seems a bit too good looking, but harmless enough as he chatters on. Sam's a darling, a cheeky chappie brimming with vim. I asked for a puppy but got two smelly wee sisters instead.

'What year are you in at school, then?' I ask.

'Don't go to school.'

'Were you expelled?' I try to hide my shock, head down, slowing.

'Nothing like that, I'm one of the good ones. Promise.'

He scarpers on up the brae. I giggle and swoop after him.

I catch him up at Ardeer Bridge. It stretches over the gully to the big house at the far end.

Showing off a bit, I say, 'This place is Old Baronial Scots.' And then to rub it in, 'I was born here.'

'Yes, I know.' We stop halfway across.

'How can you know where I was born?' The sun nips my eyes, making me squint.

'It was a maternity hospital for years. I was born here too. It's a Thin Place in Celtic Mythology, where Heaven and Earth meet.'

This sounds a bit spooky, but I don't want him to think I'm a scaredy-cat, so I say in a dismissive way, 'Imagine that.'

He stares into my eyes. 'Oh, yes, sometimes the boundary between the worlds can be crossed.'

Now, he's being ridiculous. All the same, cold fingers creep up my spine.

Glancing around, I realise I never feel entirely safe here. The old bridge crosses a narrow ravine about fifty feet deep and is built of crumbling granite, the balustrade only about four feet high with some parapets to stand in. Way below, the stream gurgles, echoing through the gully. The sun hangs high above the house. My eyes narrow against the glare, and I'm consumed by its fierce orange light. I turn my head, a half-turn, until I can see again, and gasp.

Ewan's no longer beside me on the bridge. Somehow ... I rub my eyes ... somehow, he's hovering over the balustrade, his blonde head a halo. He's beckoning me, urgency in his eyes and I'm overcome with a sense of longing. Yearning with every muscle to take his outstretched hand, I move forward and he smiles, his face lit with welcome. But I hear Granny's hushed voice. 'Get back, Gabrielle, don't go near the edge.' I stop, Ewan frowns, his eyes narrowing, his head tilted as if he too can hear her words. Forcing one foot backwards, I swivel my hips, knowing I must turn away. When I dare to look back, Ewan's fading in the sun's rays, both arms reaching out in appeal, his features tight with loss.

He disappears.

Frantic, I switch my gaze to Sam, and my heart stops as he leaps, his tail in full fan behind him, his body stretched out and fluid.

Silence encases me and I can see only a luminous violet hue ahead. I blink away tears, but the watery film doesn't shift. I press one finger into quivering air. There's a moment of resistance before sounds flood in; the rustle of trees, the cries of birds, the gurgle of the stream below, my pulsing heart.

I look to the sky, the sun swims around and around. I blink away dizziness and stumble to the end of the bridge, zigzag to the front of the house and bang the iron knocker on the great door. Maybe there's a janitor. But it's derelict, no one comes.

Inching onto the bridge again, head down against the glare, I peek down into the blackness where Sam leaped. There's no sign of him. The stream gurgles far below. A shiver runs up my back and I'm propelled helter-skelter across the bridge and downhill.

I approach my boulder, solid, real, permanent, and I slow, my chest sore, heartbeat loud in my ears. A bunch of bluebells, tied with a braid of stitched blue silk, sits on my sketchpad. When I lift the flowers, their heads dip spraying a woody scent.

I pick my way down the path and when I reach home, drop drained onto my bed.

The loud tick of my bedside clock wakes me. Exhausted and feverish, I shake off a dream about a strange boy and his dog. But I can't dislodge an image of a strange, viscous place where all is deadly silent. Mum peeks in, she's holding a glass of lemonade.

'Thank you for the bluebells, darling.' She puts the glass on my bedside table and lays her hand against my forehead. 'You've got the sun.' She pulls a blue ribbon through my fingers. 'Where did you find this?'

I've no idea. 'Must have picked it out of your knitting bag.'

'No, I haven't knitted anything blue for many a year.'

She looks away and a sliver of light picks up flecks of gold in her violet eyes. A creeping flush of recognition makes me sit up.

'Mum?'

She clasps her hand to her stomach. Takes a few short breaths to steady herself.

Alarmed, I swing my legs off the bed and sit at her side.

She presses me to her. 'I'm sorry, darling. I don't know why we never told you. We should have.'

'Told me what, Mum?' What on earth could it be? Was she ill?

'You had a twin. A brother. This is his ribbon. See, his name is stitched here.'

I finger the raised lettering. George Ewan.

She tightens her fingers around the ribbon. 'I laced it through his shawl.' She raises it to her lips and whispers, so I must lean even closer. 'He was stillborn.'

1990

Etcetera

He wis sittin on his chair, closest tae the fire, smokin like a lum, starin at the box. That stained vest got smaller specially as he got bigger, wi eatin aw they Big Macs an double chips, he'd no even take a diet coke. Too many additives'll kill ye, he said.

Well, he wis sittin on his chair, dirty vest strainin ower his belly, rolls o fat restin on his thighs, wi that wiry salt-an-pepper hair circlin his belly button, it wis enough tae gie ye the boak. He widnae buy any new claithes, no a stitch, even fer his lassie's weddin.

So's ah'm jist in frae ma work, still thinkin aboot auld Ellen. Poor auld soul hisnae got naebody else in the world, can go a whole week an no see naebody but masel. Ah take a bit o time wi her, make a wee bite an that, even if ah go ower ma hours. Ah'd left her in her curlers an jammies, aw washed, talced an fed, watchin Neighbours, a wee toatie hauf at her haun, an ah wis hopin she'd pit the tele aff when she goes tae her bed.

That night ah'm hame a bit later an ah've still got the messages tae pit away an the tea tae make, etcetera. When ah goes in, the tele's on silent, jist colours throbbin away, he's sittin on that chair wi a can o McEwans on the table wi the overflowin ashtray. Butts an ash trailin ower ma guid polished wood. His feet ur stuck oot, aw blotchy an swollen, an his soles like the dried pig's ears ye feed tae dugs. Ah tellt him he needed a chiropodist but he widnae huv it, kept sayin ah should dae his nails, big yella thick curly claws they wur tae.

Ah goes in the kitchen, pits on the totties an some broccoli, that stuff whit stinks o drains, an ah pits a mince pie in the oven. Aw this afore ah even get a pee. Bustin ah wis. Ah goes tae the toilet an grue. He did this aw the time. Didnae flush the pan. Ah hid tae clean the bowl, pour bleach aroon, an wipe aw the seat afore ah could sit doon.

So ah'm daein ma business, etcetera, when he shouts, 'Janeette, get yer airse in here.'

Noo, it wisnae that he shouted at me, ah'm used tae that. It wis the sound o it. The turn in the voice. Like he pits on this Laird an Maister fancy edge. Like it's no Janet it's Janeette, it's no arse it's airse, like he's makin a fool o me. Ah'm a patient wuman. Anybody roon here'll tell ye that ah've pit up wi a lot ower the years. Ended up in casualty many a time.

The last time wis jist afore he took no well. He wis still gettin aboot withoot the zimmer, afore he done in his hert an liver. Ah ended up in the Royal, och, wid be three years ago noo. It wis when Cheryl left the hoose, that wis the last time he pit me in the hospital. He wis oot aw night at the pub an banged the front door. Ah opens it an shush him quiet, but he kicks it shut. The dent's still in that door the day, nae amount o paint'll cover it. He comes up on me, heid doon like a bulldug, an he kicks ma shin, ma hip, ma back, an punches me in the face tae ah fall ower. Ah'm doon on the carpet when he gets behin me, on wan knee, pulls me up an starts chokin me, his fingers diggin in. 'There ye go, ye effin bitch,' he's sayin, etcetera, etcetera. Ah cannae scream, ah cannae breathe. Ah'm flailin aboot blin wi tears, an ah gets a hold o a big library book - a Catherine Cookson it wis - an it connects wi his eye. He groans, falls back, an ah scarper tae Elsie's next door. He'd cut ma heid open, ten stitches.

Ah should've listened tae oor Cheryl. She said ah should've gone tae hers. The polis wuman came, asked me tae press charges, but ah couldnae. Ah tellt her ah fell. No dobbin in ma ain man, even if he wis fond o his fists. Mainly it wisnae that bad, jist bruisin, etcetera.

Ah hoped things wid get better when he took no well. He wis tae stop the drink but he widnae, liver wis shot, the doctor said, an wan drink wid kill him. But he jist sat in that chair gettin fatter an fatter. He drank an smoked an ate. The Social gied him this extra money tae be attended tae. Ah didnae see a penny o that.

That night it wis *Janneette an airse* an when ah hurried oot the toilet, ah said, 'Yer tea's on.'

He scratches his belly, turned ma stomach that, an he looks doon his nose. 'Go oot an get me six cans,' he says.

Ah say, 'Where's aw yer pals the day?'

He calls me an effin cow, his toenails claw the carpet as he struggles tae his feet, picks up the remote an chucks it. Ah don't get oot the road fast enough. It clips me on the foreheid. Ah stumble intae the kitchen. He's no up tae bashin me, an the chair groans as he sits back doon, gruntin, 'Janet ye scrawny ugly bitch, whoare …' etcetera, etcetera.

Ah'm standin at the sink wi the teacloth at ma heid soakin up the blood. When the flow stops ah pit the cloth doon, rinse it tae the blood runs frae red, tae pink, tae clear, doon the plughole, fold it ower the drier an open the cutlery drawer.

Ah step intae the livin room, away frae the stink o broccoli. Ah've ower-cooked that, ah mutter tae masel, it'll be like rubber. He's hauf on his feet, smirk on his face, insults flyin in that posh voice, etcetera, etcetera, arms beatin air. He shuts up, looks doon, an the sneer drops, he backs away a hauf step, opens his mooth tae say somewhit. Mibbe he wis goin tae say that ah wis in the right fer a change. Ah sticks the knife in his belly, jist like cuttin butter. He flails back intae the chair, fag ash puffin aw aroon him like a shroud. He sputters, 'Ye've killt me.'

'Aye, Brendan Sweeney,' ah say, 'so ah huv.'

2012

Heron

He's here again, stencilled against the sky. He comes for the carp moping in the pond. I don't mind. We're both seeking water in this bleached out place. Shaping up to be the hottest summer in living memory in Cambridgeshire, and it's melting my synapses, swelling my ankles and making Bump feel even more of a burden. I stare at my heron. He stands still, so tall, so aloof. He'll soon beat his way over the roof to the pond. I drink him in, this gift, this reminder that there's life in this dried-up place, and think of my other visitor, the boy who came yesterday.

It was around eleven when the doorbell rang. I was wiping down the kitchen floor while sweat soaked my face. I had pulled my hair up into a ponytail but my neck itched all the same. Crabbit and tense, I swore under my breath, panicking that a neighbour was at the door and would see me in this state. I should have known better; the only visitors I had were those who came for their holidays, like Mum. I saw her newspaper-fan swishing. This was last August, when it wasn't nearly as hot.

'How can you stand the air here, Claire?' Swish-swish went the fan.

'How d'you mean?'

'It's like breathing ash. There's nae water in it.' She coughed to underline her point.

'Hardly Morocco, Mum.'

'Aye Hen, but the air's dry as dust and there isnae any hills. It's all sky and fields.'

'You know Jim can't get work in his line in Scotland.'

She lit up another cigarette and shrugged.

That was the last time I saw her. The phone call came on a Sunday morning in November. Her heart had finally given up the fight.

I flicked the lounge curtain to see a boy. He was blonde and had the thinness of the aged, but was more like seventeen. He wore shorts that showed twig legs and a straw hat that could have been Crocodile Dundee's. He was most likely a pedlar, selling door-to-door; I always felt bad that they had to do this work. I usually ended up buying clothes pegs, or last time it was an ironing board cover I didn't need and could have got cheaper in Asda. The day was tightening up and I was aware of the silence of the village. We rarely had much traffic through here; the bus came once a week, and today no farm machinery thrummed in my ear. I stepped back, but not fast enough; he spotted me and grinned from a conker face.

I unlatched the door.

'Beautiful morning, Madam.' Chalk white teeth, a cliff edge of them.

'Yes, can I help you?' Why do I always say that? I bit my lip. Tasted salt as sweat dripped off my nose.

'You like to see my work, yes?'

I was steeling myself to say that I was too busy, to go away, thanks anyway, but he beamed again and I nodded.

I noticed the portfolio leaning against the wall under the riot of ramblers. He crouched down and drew out a charcoal sketch of a woman.

'She beautiful, eh?'

'Very.'

'My mother, in Poland.'

'Yeah, right,' I thought. But actually, a closer look

showed there was a strong family likeness. 'This is very good. What's her name?'

'She was Irena.'

'My mum was called Margaret. She died …' I didn't know why I said that, but I was thinking of her again, in her pristine maisonette, Anaglypta walls fresh-painted every spring, cabinet full of Goebel figurines.

He tilted his head. 'I sorry, she no longer with you.'

Perhaps that was why I invited him in. I never do that. I'm under strict instructions from Jim to never, ever do that. But he isn't here every day, on his lonesome, killing time.

The boy clambered to the kitchen, the portfolio bouncing on his hip. I reassured myself I was five stone heavier and could squash him to death if need be.

He sat down and I padded to the fridge for the pitcher of orange, set it on the table, swiped two glasses from the shelf and sat across from him. His sapphire gaze was quite without inhibition.

I sighed. 'Let me see, then.'

He laid them out, a patchwork of faces, some in watercolours, some charcoal, some just pencilled, all with a curious energy to them, much like himself, as he rocked on the leg tucked under him.

'They good, no?' Such confidence.

'Look really fab, actually. All your own work?'

'Of course.'

He took out more, spread them on the table and I gasped. Birds. All of them. And they were in flight. I fixed on a watercolour. My bird. My grey heron.

'Ah, you like the birds?'

I picked it up; it was a heron at take-off. He'd captured the one instant when they aren't fluid; the instant when they unhinge their wings, and ratchet up vertically through the air, like the motor's cold; that moment before it catches and they sweep the sky.

'How much?' I ventured.

'How much you like?'

'How d'you mean?'

'You tell me how much you think to pay.'

Now I was bamboozled. I had no idea. 'I have ten pounds cash, that's all, but that wouldn't be enough for this intricate work.' I wiped my hands on a tea towel before tracing the feathers spread across the page.

'Sure. Deal.'

'Oh, thank you.'

'You are welcome, nice lady. When your baby come?'

'Another month.' I arched my back. Then I heard myself say, 'Would you like some food?'

'Yes, that very good.'

I fixed some sandwiches while he chattered on about Poland, and how he missed home.

'Cambridge is good, no?'

I didn't know what to say. I supposed it was rather a beautiful place really, in its own flat, dry way.

He didn't wait for my reply. 'Nice place, lots work, go back after season with plenty money. I go to the Art Academy in Gdansk.'

'Wow.' I was impressed.

He nodded, or rather sort of bowed, dipping his head to his chest. Was he laughing at me? Then serious again, he said, 'When your mother die?'

I hesitated. 'Last November, a heart attack, sudden. In Havoc, Scotland, where I come from. Your mum?'

'Yes, before Christmas.' He tilted his head in that way of his, as if he had a question: but he didn't ask it.

I picked at my sandwich; he sipped at his juice, looking out at the stretch of sun-drenched wheat. I like to imagine it's the Elvern there. It slithers into sight in a certain light, at a certain angle, running across the miles of fields: rippled blue and laced white. I paddle to my knees and splash the water upwards over my stomach, chest, face. Pebbles gleam underfoot and golden threads dart in the diamond light. Then the sun shifts and I see it's only miles of the plastic sheeting the farmers use to protect their plants. But for a moment, every time, the mirage is a miracle of sorts and I'm back at Mum's living room window, looking down the brae at the stretch of the river.

'You been here long time?' he asked.

'No. Not long enough to feel … anyway, I'm Claire.'

'Aron, how do you do?'

'Where did you see the heron?'

'Near Peterborough, the river there …the Nene. Beautiful place. Lots visitors. I see him some mornings and I watch close, then draw from memory. I like the heron, he has … what you say? Personality. He special.'

'I know, I have one too. He comes to poach the fish in the pond.'

'Clever.'

'Yes. It's as if he's been here since prehistoric times. Sometimes I think he's a pterodactyl.'

He screwed up his face.

'You know, a dinosaur.' I said, flapping my arms.

'Not changed in thousands of years. I know it.' He flapped his arms back.

I giggled. 'I like to see him, makes me feel …'

'Chosen.'

This surprised me, but he was right. 'Yes, chosen.'

'Of course, it's the way of things. We get chosen, we have no say. I need to go … someone is waiting for me.'

His stick figure trundled up the village road, portfolio swaying on his hip, until the sun swallowed him up. It was as if he had never been: another mirage.

Except for the painting.

The heron hasn't moved. I watch him as I rest my belly against the sink. I think of Mum and she scolds me. 'Buck up, Hen. Get out of this house and go find that river.'

As the bird launches from his perch and climbs skyward, wings unravelling, my baby kicks and I press my palm to the spot and say, 'C'mon you. We got someplace to go.'

2019

It Would Take a Miracle

Daisy walked briskly through the tall fretwork Havoc Cemetery gates, the traffic lulling behind her. She shifted the shopper, heavy wi bottled water and wet wipes, to her other arm. She couldnae rely on the tap here. When she was done she'd have a wee nosy at the new dug graves. After all, what was the point of those lovely flowers and cards if naebody read or enjoyed them? The deid person was past that, the kin were away home, leaving only locals and angels. Or devils depending on where you ended up. She looked to the heavens; no often she got a dry day to linger and pay respects even if it was cold and grey, the sky heavy wi gloom.

Anyway, she was glad to be out the house as her heart was roasted wi aw they forms. Annoying that the Department of Work and Pensions had to send them, couldnae pick them up at the Post Office. They said to phone in your application but she was nae guid on the phone, couldnae follow what was being said and aye mucked it up. But twenty-eight pages?

She might no bother applying at aw.

Just starve to death, be found skin and bone on the kitchen floor.

Doctor Kane was a lovely man, insisted she apply, even though she tellt him she wouldnae get anything. 'I'm no sick. It's aw in the heid, Son,' she said. 'I can walk, cook and clean so I can still work, don't need nae Personal Independence Payments.'

Och, they were poor souls here, a few new ones the day, nae heidstones yet, easy to spot wi their carpet of flowers. The bright colours drew her eye past the drab stones, the dirt, the grass. She smiled, it was guid to spit in the eye of death.

The silence was pierced by the shrill cries of gulls overhead and the lament of a dove. No a soul around. The gravediggers were usually about, having a fag, leaning on their spades. No a job Daisy'd like, though it depended on how you looked at it. You could take the view you were digging graves or take the other view you were a gardener planting, cutting grass, or landscaping. No digging in the daytime, mind. They did that early morning, then covered the open grave wi a bright green tarpaulin. She might just get cremated and save a lot of carry-on.

She gathered herself and ambled around the corner to her mam and da's grave where she dropped her bag, leant doon and took out a bunch of droopy red peonies, the water bottle and her antiseptic wet wipes. After a wee clean-up of the stone and a change of the water in the vase it was aw hunky-dory. Except the lettering looked dull. She knelt in front of the stone wi a pot of Brasso and a cloth and rubbed the letters until they shone.

Thank God for wet wipes and bottled water. And Brasso, of course.

She stood up straight. 'Mam, you were poor aw your days, but I don't remember you ever had to rely on the government or go to a food bank for your dinner. Last Monday I hung about so long in the rain I was fair soaked when I went in that door. There arenae the shifts at work. My wages clear ran out.' She made a slow sign of the cross. 'Bye Mam and Da. See you next time.'

Daisy stepped along the path, turned right, and zigzagged through some gravestones, 'Sorry, sorry,' until she spotted the Scots Pine that sheltered Alec and the wean. 'Nae tears,

Daisy. It's aw so long ago, but also no so long ago. A well-kept grave, wouldnae have it any other way.'

She cleaned the black panel, polished the lettering, picked off spots of damp, got up off her knees, gripping the curved edge of the gravestone, and brushed away dirt and grass from her slacks. Her heid bowed, she made the sign of the cross. 'See you next time, my darlings.'

Today she felt like lingering, so decided on a wee saunter in the auld lanes where rich folk were buried under big heidstones adorned wi angels and cherubs. Slowing to a stop, she peered at a grubby angel, years of green mould running down the legs and ower her cherubic face. Her wings were black wi it. Daisy supposed there was naebody left to clean it up. She moved in closer. Aye, a few of them in there. Woolfries, Mary-Anne, six months of age. Died in 1937. And a brother, Nicholas, died age seven months, and two more infants. Bless that poor mother, she was there too. 1945. And a father, 1960. Heartache came whether or no you were rich.

Hey, that was fair annoying the state of that angel. She could clean the wee face if she stood on that tree trunk. What did folk do in the auld days before wet wipes? Aye, her mother had auld rags in bleach constantly. Choking smell through the house aw day long. Probably where Daisy got her obsession, as Alec had called it. *Daisy stop cleaning, the place is like an operating theatre.*

'Order and cleanliness are what keeps us alive,' she'd replied.

What was that there? Och, only a wee robin perched on the angel's heid. So tame, those birds. But this one had shat aw doon the angel's face. Bugger. 'Shoo, shoo.' It hopped away, miffed. 'Shoo, shoo …' He was flying away, no … landed ontae the next stone waiting for her to leave. She wasnae going nowhere. That would definitely need cleaned up now.

Daisy stepped on the grass, climbed ontae the tree trunk, leant ower, rubbed the angel's face, and scrubbed again. The surface was warm under her fingers, no like stone at aw. And they flecks on the face wouldnae rub off, no matter how hard Daisy scrubbed. They couldnae be? Aye, freckles. That was awfy clever of the stonemason. The stone ringlets had a tone of red about them. Hardly, must've been the sun. But there wasnae any sun, just grey sky up there. Maybe a lamp was shining some place. The eyes were like sapphires, glass of course. Mind, that was unusual on a statue?

It had lashes, fair and silken. Brushed the back of Daisy's hand like a whisper. She drew it back fast.

Christ almighty, the statue was yawning. Daisy cried out, 'Get doon, quick. Oh my, I must be hallucinating. It's they tablets.' She backed away, stepped off the trunk, and tottered to the bench to rest a minute.

Phew, she was away wi the fairies. The doc was right. There, the angel was back to what she was. A statue. Daisy's heart drummed, the form business had been too much. Two or three shifts would do her, there was aye the food bank if she got stuck again.

She took a peek, it was just a statue.

A loud bang, what the Hell?

Gravestones shook, tarmacadam cracked, a deep rumble ran underfoot.

The angel shivered, fluttered, her wings quivered, unfolded but strained as if stuck. She flexed arms, shoulders, stretched her neck. A squeak, a rattle, crumbling cement, a crack on the plate, dust flying, and the heidstone split in half. Now, a sharp snap like breaking bone; the feet were loose from the plate, the wings spreading and …

Daisy screamed, 'Doon, Daisy doon. Watch your heid. She's up, she's away.'

Blinking uncontrollably, Daisy lay on her side on the bench. 'There, there. No, still gone. The angel's gone.'

Only crumbling cement, cracks, and choking dust remained.

Daisy sat up, coughed, spat, fumbled in her bag for baby wipes and wiped dirt from her face.

The rumbling underfoot had stopped. She tried to get up on her feet but her legs were water. 'Maybe God didnae like me walking on the graves. Sorry, sorry, in the name of the Father, the Son, the Holy Ghost …' Where was everyone? How come no one had heard the noise? The place was still deserted, though Daisy's vision was clouded, and she couldnae see more than a few yards around her.

Out of the fog of dust came a friendly voice. 'Hello.'

Daisy turned from side to side. 'Oh hello, I'm so glad to see a living soul. Mother of God …' It was her off the plinth. Daisy's heart raced but paralysis stayed her joints and it was a long way to the safety of the main road.

The angel perched down beside her on the bench. Daisy slid away as far as she could; the wings took up a lot of space and Daisy wasnae for soiling that delicate stuff.

She was put in mind of sitting on a bus beside a drunk, trying to pretend you werenae there, ignoring the fact the drunk was stinking. Though this angel smelt like freesia petals. Daisy glanced ower, och no, the wee soul was greetin.

Daisy fished in her pocket and held out the pack of baby wipes. The angel reached for it wi graceful fingers, and extracted one, two, three. Daisy tore off the last one for her. How pretty the wee thing was, pale and slender. But that might've been an illusion as she was hovering now in front of the bench, feet off the ground, wings fluttering either side: feathery blues, pinks, and greens displacing what remained of the settling smog. The angel dried her eyes and handed Daisy the wipes. Stuffing them in her bag, Daisy leant hard against the bench. The cemetery was deathly quiet, no sign of the robin, no dove calls, no even any seagulls or ravens.

Just Daisy and an angel, an angel woken wi a wet wipe.

Daisy wondered what she could've done wi a bottle of Domestos. 'How did you manage to get off that pedestal, Hen?'

'You freed me.'

'Me?'

'Yes, you showed me a kindness.' She perched on the arm of the bench, wings at rest.

'So, like rubbing a lamp. Are you a genie?'

She giggled, tears forgotten. 'Not at all, I'm an angel. Seraphim, to be exact.'

Daisy remembered something about seraphims from her catechism; they were pals wi cherubims. Guid angels. 'Very nice.'

This was a wee bit embarrassing. The angel probably wasnae there and Daisy'd be caught talking to hersel. The doc was right and she should apply for that PIP benefit. If she put this hallucination on the form, she'd qualify no bother. She closed her eyes, and blinked them open slowly. The angel was still there. If she wasnae real, Daisy'd best get on, ignore the vision. If she was real, then she'd best get on. Dragging hersel up, she said, 'Nice to meet you, I'll be on my way now.'

Walking towards the gates, Daisy didnae look back, but wing vibration stirred the air behind her, from one side to the other. The angel swung out in front of Daisy's face and hovered, stopping her in her tracks. Dipping her heid the seraphim said, 'Thank you, Daisy,' and disappeared.

Daisy's heart sank, jumped, sank again. She'd better go home before she collapsed or saw devils. Just as she exited the big gates there was a commotion. Three cemetery workers bashed out of their yard, one on his phone. 'There's been an explosion. Fire brigade, aye. A grave's blown up, aye aye …'

Daisy put a step on it.

When she reached her house, she clinked the gate and

walked up the path, unlocked the front door and let hersel in. A nasty shock greeted her in the lobby mirror. Her face and shoulders were caked in white dust and blood streaked her foreheid. She fingered her hairline: a cut nipped but it had stopped bleeding.

She stepped on some envelopes, leant doon, and picked them up. One looked official. Inside was a letter. *Mrs Riley, you have been awarded the high rate of Personal Independent Payment, payable into your bank account from ...*

She let it flutter to the table.

2019

Next Stop

It's packed in here, plenty thin folk, naebody burling drunk and nae smoking allowed. No a seat tae spare. Waiting Room 4. A rectangle cut oot of the corridor, nae doors. The woman opposite looks awfy poorly, must be in her eighties, poor auld soul ending up here on the edge of her seat, gripping her Zimmer frame. Looks like she's had her hair done, a perm and blue rinse, disnae offset her rheumy eyes. Och, and the rings on her bony fingers have rolled doon tae her swollen knuckles. That'll be her carer on the next seat, eyes stuck tae the *People's Friend,* but she cannae be reading as she keeps switching her wrist tae see the time, and she's turning the pages too fast. The rustle gets on yer nerves. I wish she'd pay her charge a bit of attention or the auld dear'll feel she's a burden.

It's a lottery wi us carers these days. They dinnae know who they'll get, or even if it'll be the same one who rushes up the stairs at teatime who fed them at breakfast, likely at half past six, dragging them oot of their bed. It never used tae be like that. Cuts, cuts, cuts. I gie the auld lady a wee smile, one of them ye can turn intae a cough if it's no reciprocated. It's no, so I cough but my throat's tight and it turns intae a bit of a choke, and everybody else starts up, but the auld lady disnae stir.

The young fella at the end of the row's here aw by hissel. He keeps fiddling wi his ticket, dropped it twice awready.

He looks healthy, slim, guid-looking, nae signs of drink, no a smoker. Maybe he's on the drugs. Naw. Too well turned oot. Clean shaven, ironed shirt. Nae wedding ring. I want tae tell him tae keep an eye on the screen, ye need tae keep watching tae see yer number come up, but he keeps his head doon, taps his foot on the beige vinyl. That stuff goes aw the way through the hospital. Easy cleaned wi they big buffer machines. The place is spotless, even the loos. Nice scent of bleach.

I peek up at the two other women in the queue; they look in their sixties, both wi their other halves. Aye, the women are the sick ones. Ye can see it in their eyes, even withoot the clutched tickets. They blink too much. Mind, it's no exactly a spa experience, the owerhead lights are awfy bright for a start, and the place is busy wi staff milling aboot in they green and blue scrubs. And trainers on their feet. I suppose they dae a lot of walking. They come and go, the slap of soles, breaking intae the quiet. Some drift by, some race, others push trolleys full of files. Heavy work, that. Us here on the seats and them in their blues or greens, wheeling trolleys and carrying files. Oor files. The ones sitting here wi their other halves. If my other half hadnae legged it twenty years ago, he'd be here holding my hand. But I wish I had taken somebody, noo I'm here wi aw these sick folk. Jessie would've come if I'd asked her, but och she's no well. What wi her arthritis and her psoriasis, and the other day she's telling me she's been diagnosed wi insomnia. Hypochondria tae my mind. She'd be no use here, gie her ideas.

Must be my turn soon, they go in and oot fast. Expert blood takers here, so many tae dae. No like Doctor Kane doon at the health centre. Black-and-blue I was last time, but I said tae him, 'It's awright Son, ye've no got the everyday experience.' Naw, he's no like these nurses here. Lovely lassies, so they are. Treat ye like royalty. Course, I'd rather no be here at aw. When ye're here there's no escaping it.

Most of the time I can pack it away in a cardboard box in the dark of my wardrobe. That nice counsellor lady I saw, och, twenty years ago noo, after my man left me, taught me how tae imagine stuff away. Ye dinnae need tae see it or think aboot it. But when ye're here it's public knowledge. No hiding. Ye cannae pretend ye've got a sore throat, or piles, or a bad cough here. Ye're stripped bare. Forced tae imagine aw sorts. Like my gravestone. *Here lies the woman wi the stopper in her gob who couldnae ask The Question.*

Oops, my number's up. My ticker's on the trot, I want it done, but I want it no tae come. Sometimes I wonder if my heart will stand it in the end. I raise my ticket, in case I get accused of jumping the queue, and shuffle aroon the coffee table, *sorry sorry sorry* ... Cannae help but step on toes.

I follow the arrows tae another cubby hole. The nurse, a happy looking chappy wi one of they buzz cuts, grins as he settles me intae a chair, checks my number, asks my name and date of birth. He picks something off his tray. I turn away; he tells me it'll be cold, that's the wipe. Then his fingers rub the skin, get the vein up. A prick, his breath fills the room. I've stopped breathing. Then he bellows a 'well done'. As if I've done something special, gied him a guid vein, didnae faint ...

I forgot tae ask what the blood test's for. Should've brought somebody wi me tae ask that stuff. Yer mind's racing or blank and ye can only catch the gist of it aw, no the detail. Mind, that'd mean telling the family. They'd go off on one, have me at death's door. Specially my Mary. I'd end up making her tea and calming her doon. Anyhows, I never get a word in edgeways, *how ye doin Mum?* and then as soon as ye open yer mouth they've turned away, or they're on their phones ... I should go intae the street and bawl it oot. That might make them stop for a minute. I imagine Jessie, Mary, and Pete in black at the funeral service. What would they say aboot me? Loved her family, worked hard aw her days, guid clean-living woman. Aye, aw that. Hasnae done me any guid. Nae pension tae speak of; the government stole that and I willnae get it until I'm sixty-six. If I make sixty-six wi the cleaning jobs, the carer shifts, and no seeing the same auld soul from one shift tae the next. Should've gone tae Disney World, Florida, wi Mary and the weans. Just the once.

Noo Waiting Room 5. Another rectangular seating affair. Nae tickets but. My name's called. A young doctor peeks oot of a door tae my left, a half smile on his face. I get up, inch aroon the table. I'm getting better at missing feet. He waves me through the door. We sit doon at a desk wi a computer and files. He introduces hissel but I dinnae catch the name. It's on the blue tag on the ribbon roon his neck, but it's hanging doon ower his belly and I dinnae like tae stare.

He peers intae his screen and says, 'Mrs Muir, your date of birth?'

'Call me Elsie. Have ye no got that there, Son?'

'Just so I know for sure who you are.'

'Oh, right, twentieth October.'

'And the year?'

'Nineteen fifty-eight.'

'Address?'

'Twelve Alcluith Street, Havoc, Flat two, stroke one. Second floor, on the right as ye come up the stair.'

'So ...'

Aw the kids start their sentences wi *so* these days. *So* this and *so* that. It disnae mean anything. He's stock-still ... staring intae the screen.

'So?' I ask.

He sighs.

A bolt of fright zips through me. 'Bad news then?'

'It's a large tumour,' he says, and talks aboot some stage, and mentions numbers.

Course, I knew it was cancer. Wouldnae be here

otherwise. But I dinnae catch what it is exactly, in-between him chewing his lip and staring at the picture on the screen, a hairball, aw matted and glued up against what looks like a wall. Black-and-white, tae. Ye'd think they'd have colour. But the NHS is fair strapped for cash. It's aw they hip and knee replacements folk dinnae need.

He shifts roon in his chair. Looks at me wi doe brown eyes. 'As I said, it is … a third stage cancer … but we can look after you.'

I say, 'Guid news then?'

He's befuddled, closes his eyes tight. Maybe he's just tired. Poor lad. He gets oot a sheet of paper wi questions. We go through and he ticks the boxes.

No smoking.

No alcohol … well just a couple gins on a Saturday.

Not obese.

No allergies. No high blood-pressure. No medications.

'So,' he says, 'you're fit and healthy otherwise.' He smiles, pleased. I'm pleased he smiled, so I smile back.

He fishes in a drawer, gies me a leaflet. Taps intae his computer, a swishing noise rises behind me. We both turn. He gets up, lifts two pages from the printer, one a prescription for the GP. He passes it tae me. I slip it in my bag. He offers his hand. I shake it.

'Thank you, Doctor.'

I hesitate at the door. I havenae asked *The Question.*

He looks up, surprise on his face. I'm supposed tae be gone. 'Yes, can I help you with anything else?'

Och, I dinnae like tae bother him so I ask another question. 'Did I dae something tae bring this on?'

'Not at all. Everyone's different, risks, vulnerabilities, genetic make-up.'

I'm almost oot, draw masel up, turn back, open my mouth tae ask *The Question,* but he's awready stuck on his computer.

Walking along corridors, following arrows tae the exit, I'm in another world. People in wheelchairs, on sticks, skeletons who look sucked dry. A man wi skin like yellow crepe hobbles past me. I reach the café, could dae wi a cuppa, my throat's vice tight, but dinnae want tae linger. I'm no like them. Like the doc said, I'm fit and well. Someone laughs, a hearty guffaw. The woman serving teas smiles broadly. I step ootside, follow the red path past the car park, and cross the road tae the bus stop. It's tempting tae walk further, get on at the next stop but I hesitate. An auld woman stands there alone. She nods. I take up my place, second in the queue.

'Busy in there, isn't it?' she says.

'Aye, couldnae wait tae get oot the place.'

'You'll get used to it,' she says. 'I've been going there for five years.'

I hope I'll be going there for five years.

She pats my arm, tilts her head, holds my gaze, oor eyes well up. She offers me a barley sugar. It soothes my throat. We dinnae say anything else. The bus rolls up and we get on it thegither.

2019

Blackbird

A bird's call of alarm scythed into Archie's brain. He pulled the duvet over his head and flickered his eyes open. His legs were bone stiff, like an auld man's, and he still the guid side of seventy. Morning seeped in through the curtains, puddling at the door like sour milk. He pressed the button at the top of the clock, quarter past seven glowed ghostly green. He inched his legs over the side of the bed and forced himself up.

Damn blackbird was still at it. Archie felt for his loafers and shoved them on, but couldn't pass Ruby's side without easing himself down again. The duvet was flat, undisturbed, her pillows plump shadows. Leaning over, he tapped her lamp's base till it blinked on, then off, tapped harder several times till it steadied. He stared at the empty space. She always slept on her left side, her hips spooned into his middle, her hand curled under her cheek. She'd no be coming home now. Was a blessing, the nephew said.

Archie winced at the pincers in his knees, and shuffled down the hall to the kitchen, pressing switches as he passed. The bungalow had been their project for the past two years and they'd done a guid job. It was as she liked it, modern and sleek with plain lines. She never was a fussy woman.

Only a few months ago, she was bustling about, blue eyes flashing, lips pursed, nagging him about one thing or the other.

'Archie, ye'll miss the bin men again.'
'Archie, ye'll need tae clear that drain.'
'Archie, get tae fixing that tap before I clout ye.'

Och, she was never really annoyed with him. Always had a kiss or a warm word to smooth things over.

They'd had plans but what was the point of hard physical labour now? Ruby wasn't there to keep the teapot on the simmer and the bacon butties crisp, to tell him off and to keep him right.

Ever since that time, she'd kept him right.

They'd been scraping along in the room-and-kitchen near the docks, an outside cludgie on the half-landing, a ring of ice under your arse in winter. He was bricklaying then, twelve quid a week, for auld skinflint McDougall.

Archie turned the tap on and the water splashed up, missing the kettle's spout. He started again. Light was angling through the vertical blinds in the lounge next door, picking out the amber bottle and crystal tumbler from last night. After he flicked on the toast, he realised he'd forgotten to take the butter out of the fridge and he had to dig it out in clods. Ruby's toast was always perfect, light caramel with golden streaks, while his looked like sick on tar. And her tea was hot and sweet. His was always too strong and bitter. It was his timing that was always out.

He sat at the modern breakfast bar, smoothed his hand over the cool expanse of the marble worktop and shivered. The heating was on, and April just around the corner. It must be shock. The shock of hearing the words yesterday and Daniel on the phone last night. 'No worries, Uncle Archie. You fish out your marriage certificate and Auntie's birth certificate and I'll do the rest from here.'

Archie raised the cremated toast to his mouth but stopped mid-chin. Best fish out the certificates, then. They'd be in the auld suitcase her mother had given her when they married. She kept all the documents in there. He looked up at the ceiling, envisioning the loft, how the rafters spread and the joists held. The case was on top of the box of ornaments that she'd packed but hadn't thrown away.

He made his way down the hall to the ceiling hatch, got out the lever and pushed. The ladder screeched down and he climbed up into the loft space. They had plans to convert it to a bedroom. For when the grandnieces came, Ruby said, but they wouldn't come now. He crouched until he reached the apex and could stand tall, wheeled around and located the case, its brown leather handle drooping, it's check cloth smudged with age and dust. He lifted it up, it was heavy, but he was still strong. Building work had hardened the muscles in his arms and chest even if it had knackered his knees. He balanced the case on top of the ladders as he swerved onto a lower rung, but as he hauled it down, the bottom snapped out, plunging all the paper in a shower over his head. He was left with only the ruptured case, now feather light. Leaning his frame against the hard steel ridges, he splayed his feet on a lower step, and closed his eyes, blinking away the salt nip before starting his descent, only to stop at a headline splayed across a middle rung. He picked up the yellowed newspaper page.

20-Year-Old-Man Held for Questioning in Rape Case.

Archie crushed it in his fist. He should've known she'd have kept all this. He eased onto the floor and gathered up the papers, shovelling them back in the case. He carried it to the kitchen, the split side at his hip, heaved it up on the worktop, picked out any papers about that time, ripped them to pieces and pushed them down into the bin.

The polis had come on a Sunday night. October it was. And a hard winter on them. The wind blew the rain against the windows and swung about the building like a ghoul. They were fixing to finish the dishes when the door banged. They'd no heard anyone on the stairwell on account of the weather so both jumped. Archie answered and before he could register the uniforms, he was manhandled and cuffed against the tiled wall. As he was half-hauled, half-marched down the stairs all he could see, his neck craned, was Ruby's wide eyes and the O of her mouth.

Ruby had saved him back then. She'd written her letters by hand, that upright, neat handwriting. Took carbon paper copies. Made sure he had the best brief. Without hesitation she'd stood in that box and in her soft way, her wide-eyed innocence, told the judge why he couldn't have done it. Archie's torso tightened from neck to thigh. He'd have turned mad in gaol if it hadn't been for Ruby.

He thought there'd be time to make up to her. But she never demanded anything. No cruises or foreign trips, just a wee drive down to Largs for a pokey-hat or up the Loch to see the forest split the water on a summer's day. She knew he didn't like changes in routine. He sat down and slurped his tea, remembered the certificates, found a buff envelope and took a moment to trace their names on the marriage papers before forcing them inside. He closed the suitcase, found some tape and patched it up. Jobs to be done. He'd start that reading room she'd asked about. Dig an eight by ten patch for it in the garden. No that she'd been doing much reading lately but it would be nice to sit in.

He hadn't wanted to believe it. No his clever girl who looked after him, sorted out his building business, done two jobs herself to keep them afloat till he'd got on his feet. Nobody would take a chance on him. Ruby said he should work for himself and he did, made a guid living too over the years, no big projects, he hadn't the head for that, but he'd got his City and Guilds with her help. She did her caring work and cleaning. What were they called in those days? Aye, home helps. Those days they did everything from shopping to wiping arses. Ruby could have done with one of them.

He'd go out and dig her that foundation.

The day was settling to be a guid yin. Archie pulled on his work clothes in the hall where he kept them in the auld coal bunker. The garden had been left to run its own way. A line of hedges zigzagged all the way to the back wall, overwhelming the path. An apple tree, gnarled and covered with fungus, needed treating to help it recover. One side of the plot was under water from the winter, but would dry out by next month. At the back there was a peaceful spot that got most of the sun where she could sit and read or just look out at the garden once it was made nice for her. He took his spade and securing the rim under his boot he twisted and forced it into the ground, past resistant weeds and long grass, into velvet smooth soil. He made his way left, turning at a right angle to carve out the rough shape of where the foundation would go. As he worked, the birds sang in the hedges and once he stopped to follow a flight of geese honking high in the sky in a V procession. It wasn't until his stomach groaned and he laid the spade on the grass, that he noticed the blackbird. It was silent now, just stood there, a few feet back, watching him, with those orange-ringed eyes. Pinning him as though weighing him up. Deciding if he could be trusted. Archie took a step towards him, the bird held its ground. He took another and it spread its wings just enough to slither over the grass to one side. Archie passed him and by the time he reached the kitchen door the bird had moved to the dirt patch and was stabbing his beak into worm heaven. The bird stayed with him the rest of the day, only flying off every now and then with a beak full of wriggling food. It got closer, almost under his feet once or twice. Aye, he was a plucky character.

His Ruby was a plucky lass, and she also had brains. No schooling mind, but she was a reader. The shelves were groaning with her Mills & Boons and her magazines. Loved a guid story did his Ruby and sometimes she'd read one out to him in bed in that little trill she had for reading. Only if she found a guid one about a working man, or a fella on his uppers. The books kept her going those days when she had no one else to talk to, when folk turned their backs in the street.

She'd changed, though. Aye, became more suspicious of folk, said you couldn't take them at face value. She was ambitious too. 'No reason we shouldn't have the best in life. We've nothing to be ashamed of.' Archie wasn't ashamed, but Ruby had been. Felt the shame of people sniggering behind their backs. It was the verdict that done it.

The moment the jury spokesman had said it, Archie swung around to his lawyer. He didn't know, for sure, if it was a guid or bad thing. The chap had jowls and bulging eyes like a toad, but he was nodding and smiling. Archie looked up at the gallery searching for Ruby's face but she was frowning at the jury box. She caught his eye and smiled then, so he knew it was awright. *Free to go* the judge said, his face dark, his voice stern. Archie only worked it all out later. He wasn't guilty but neither was he proved innocent. He was Not Proven.

By the time dusk crept over the garden, Archie had dug out the rectangle he needed and filled five sacks of weeds for the dump. The blackbird must've eaten a ton of worms. It was time to get cleaned up. At the sink, he stripped to his waist, soaped his hands, arms and chest till the dirt slewed away and then took his shower.

Ruby would say, 'Mind and wash off the dirt before ye get in that shower.'

'Lass, what d'ye think I put it in for?'

'To wash in, of course, but no to clog the drain wi sand and cement.'

'I've no got cement on my skin, woman.'

'It's in yer bones.'

She always got the better of him. The business would

never have got off the ground if it wasn't for her. She'd kept it small, only the occasional apprentice. Extensions, bathrooms, kitchens, nothing too taxing. Archie stood under the shower and turned up the heat till it stung his shoulders. He thought about the bullies at school and at work. How Auld McDougall had picked on him. Till he took a late growth spurt and learned to talk back with his fists. But that all stopped with Ruby. Even so, McDougall couldn't wait to point the finger.

Archie towelled dry and padded into the bedroom. It was nearly full dark and that bird was screeching like a banshee. Jab, jab, jab, into his brain. Something had been circling in there all day. He couldn't quite catch it. Ruby would have known.

He'd have to get a move on if he was to be at the hospital by visiting time. There was a pack of digestives in the biscuit tin he was keeping for her and he stuck it in a plastic bag with the buff envelope, double checked the house was locked and got in the car. The journey went by in a flash and he joined all the other worried faces through corridor after corridor until he reached her ward. He loitered at the empty nurses' station for a few minutes but nobody came so he went on to Ruby's room.

His wee Ruby, the hairstyle she took pains to keep nice, matted in grey strings at the back of her head, muttering to herself, the skin on her hands paper thin. The Team, they called themselves, all in it together, telling him he couldn't have her home, that he couldn't manage her. That social worker woman talking slow as if he was an idiot, telling him to bring in the documentation for the file.

He stroked Ruby's warm hand and she smiled at him. She knew him tonight. He put the biscuits on the shelf and they sat together for the hour, her dozing, him thinking. When the bell rang, he kissed her forehead and she blinked several times.

Ruby needed round the clock care, the social worker said. Aye, that meant sending her to one of they homes where she wouldn't know a soul. Where she'd be frightened and all alone.

Archie held the plastic bag with the documents tight to his chest, and made sure to look straight ahead as he strode past the nurses' station and out of the hospital.

2023

Passing Places

If that eejit thinks I'm gonna move he's got another thing coming. Even if his shiny new Range Rover is bigger than my wee van, I'm no shifting. He can back up and let me pass.

But no, he's ramming the horn; its shrieks fair bellow around these cliffs. Now he's mouthing out of the window, hand waving at me to reverse. Oh, you want a fight, do you, arsehole? Just let me get that length of copper pipe out of the back. Making faces now? Righto.

Jeez, I thought folk would be more friendly here; I wonder what the locals think about tourists like him acting as if they own the place. He looks like he's got a lightning rod up his arse sparking his face crimson.

I slide open the driver's door and step down, reach back in and come out swinging my length of pipe. Beetroot-face rolls up his window in a hurry, shock paralysing his ugly mug. Didnae expect that, mister. Thought I was just a wee lassie you could bully off the road. He backs up the Range Rover and I throw the pipe into the van wi a clang and slip behind the wheel. He's inched the car into a wedge cut out of the hillside beside a sign that says *passing place*. I give his disgusted mug a wide grin as my van groans past him.

This road's something else, but. Mrs Sat Nav said nothing about a vertical gradient or a single-track road, just to turn left on the trunk road and drive eight mile. My van's struggling its way up here in second gear and I'm struggling to keep my sweaty hands on the wheel.

I should just chuck Grannie out here and turn around, go back downhill, onto the main road, and back across the Skye bridge, go home to Havoc where I belong. But a promise is a promise. And her stories keep leaping onto the windscreen like a film; shots of shingle beaches, uncles and grandpas in rolled-up trousers, rainbow painted fishing boats laden wi mackerel, crab and lobster, barn dances wi girls doing the twist in dirndl skirts and nineteen-fifties perms. Aye, sunsets and sunrises and the peace of long purple gloamings.

I climb up and up, praying I don't meet another vehicle. There are places here that are a vertical drop if you were to stray off the road an inch, though the view is awright. Maybe a bit too countryside for me wi aw that purple heather, yellow gorse, and they clumps of wool plastered to the hillside like wads of white candyfloss. More sheep than people on this island, so Grannie used to say. 'The Misty Isle, Island of Wings, ma hame,' she'd spout when she'd had a wee hauf, which wasnae often, maybe a Saturday night.

She'd get maudlin at times and tell me aw about Skye where her mother, Great-Grannie Isla came from. She'd talk of faeries and wise women, the Cuillin mountains and how Skye was once a land of giants. How the Auld Man of Storr was a slain giant swallowed up by the land until only his thumb remained in sight. She'd spin tales about Skye's mischievous faeries who'd trick human beings into shady deals. 'Watch oot for them, Morven.' And about the Brownies, who helped crofters and weavers. 'They'll be pals if ye let them.' She'd tell of how a visit to the faerie pools would heal aw ailments. A bit late for that now, Grannie. The chance for healing has passed you by.

I'd often remind her, 'But Grannie ye've never been to Skye, yersel.'

They werenae her memories, they were her mother's

memories that she kept warm.

We were aye going, next year she'd have some extra cash, or the next, but it never happened. Though she almost made it that time when she was just about to step on the bus after saving up a whole year, and her neighbour came running to tell her Ishbel was in the Royal Infirmary after another fall. The bus, and the opportunity, passed her by then too.

Many times, she'd grip my wrist when I was picking up her tumbler for a refill and say, 'You promise me, Morven, Hen, when I go, ye've tae scatter ma ashes on the Misty Isle.'

So, here we are. A promise made is a promise kept.

My eyes are smarting again. I glance at the heather and thistles decorating the tube peeking out of the canvas bag on the passenger seat. Six weeks she's been gone, and I miss her sorely. It doesnae feel real, I'm still in the same house, and her room looks the same wi the flowery bedding and aw they candles on the sideboard.

Och Grannie, I want you back. How am I gonnae manage Ishbel by masel?

Thank God, here I am at last, coming down the hill. She'd have loved this. The water is just gleaming, so it is. I understand now what she meant wi aw that talk of faeries. I can see them clearly now. It's like they're dancing on the sea. A great big blue dancehall of dazzling sequins.

And more sheep on the slopes leading to the water. Imagine Great-Grannie Isla living here. I thought we were just Havoc folk born and bred. Welders, cooks, cleaners and the odd junkie and alcoholic. And me, the first proper tradesperson in the family. But, no, Grannie said we were crofters and weavers first. Turfed off the land to make room for these blasted sheep, some of us travelling to the end of the world, others sinking into poverty in the Central Belt.

Grannie hold on, we're exiting this highway in the sky, and we're turning onto a coastal road. There it is, a sign for the village. We're almost there.

*

The cottage was easy to find, given that there's only about a dozen croft houses in the bay, some of them just ruins, brick, stone, and nae roofs. Nae windows either, like eyeless trolls. But this one's been done up nice. Guid fittings in the bathroom, top end Mira shower. The toilet seat's a bit shaky but the place is no bad for the money. Mind it's out of season. The heating works, there's a top end Worcester boiler, and there's a guid enough cooker and microwave in the mezzanine kitchen. It's aw been modernised wi slate tiled floors and the rafters on show like you see in those Scandinavian houses. Lots of black-and-white photos of auld-fashioned folk; farmers, fishermen, crofters. And there's a map of the island on the wall, wi Storr, and the faerie pools marked.

Here's a notice about how to deal wi midgies — you cannae — and a kit to pick the wee bastard tick mites out of your skin. The bedroom's down the stairs. I hope Grannie doesn't mind that I've put her on the coffee table across from the tele. I'd place her on the windowsill to see the water sparkling in the sun but the windows are aw facing the hillside, the back of the cottage to the sea. Probably for shelter. The only window, where you can see the water and the bay, is in the roof up in the kitchen mezzanine. It's hypnotic, I could stand there forever, it draws you in. Wi the window open, the sound of the waves splashing and breaking on the rocks comes right into the cottage.

Grannie, you were more like my mum aw they years, working your fingers to the bone to make sure I had chances to get on and no end up like my mother, aye scraping up enough cash or favours to keep hersel in tinnies and weed.

I'm feeling a bit tired now Grannie, so I'm just gonna pull this cosy green tartan blanket around me and have a wee nap.

Stay wi me Grannie while I sleep.

*

Across from me, Grannie sits on the rocking chair by the fire, hands folded on her lap, nodding softly as she rocks back and forth.

'Grannie, I want you back, I miss you.'

'Hen, ye know I'll aye be wi ye. In yer memories and in yer dreams, and sometimes in the atmosphere aw aroon ye.'

'But I want you real, warm and alive.'

'It's your turn now, Morven, my darlin. Your life's ahead tae make of what ye will. It's the way of it, the dead pass on tae make room for the new. You're walking one way and me the other.'

This is what worries me. 'I don't know what to do.'

'Och aye, ye dae. Don't ye feel it, Hen? The pull of this place.'

'I cannae leave her.'

'Aye ye can. An ye must. It's time ye looked efter yersel.' Grannie smiles and as I blink masel awake, she fades away.

*

I turn the shower up to max, enough to feel the searing heat but no enough to burn. Just what I need after a fitful night. After drying off, I dress in my chinos, thick socks and warmest jumper. Funny, but that dream of Grannie seemed right real. I've tried hard no to let sad thoughts get to me but they come in dreams anyway. It was nice to see her sitting there so real. She looked snug and happy in this place. She might've been right about this island being her true home. It'd been calling her for years. I'm glad I brought her. Somehow, I seem more settled too.

Anyway, I've gret too much awready. Working up a sweat, fitting a kitchen or bathroom usually sorts me out, but here, there's just peace, quiet and space. Except for the blowing of the wind and the sound of the sea sloshing out there against the shore. No that there's much of a shore; it's no like Spain here, no Riviera, just rocks and shingle as far as I can see, though the guidebook said there are sands someplace. Exploring can come later when the job's done. Then and only then will I look for those faerie pools.

This morning sunshine dapples the windows. Might be a guid time to do the business. Throw Grannie into the sea where she wants to be.

My mobile breaks the silence. My stomach churns when I see Ishbel's name. I don't want to answer. She knows I'm here on this job and I tellt her I wouldnae be around for a few days. I could throttle her. She knows I'll aye answer because I'd feel bad if anything happened to her. Reluctantly, I pick it up and put it on speaker phone. 'Hello, Mum.'

The whining, throaty voice replies. 'Morven, when will ye be back? That carer woman isnae any guid. She's trying to make me walk to the toilet and I cannae dae that, ye know I cannae.' The voice starts to break up, the usual tears will start soon.

I don't feel sympathy, just annoyance, then a pang of guilt as I shouldnae feel like that.

'Mum, I'm sure she's trying to help. She's a nice woman …'

Ishbel interrupts. 'Naw she's no. I sent her on her way, I don't need carers, I'm no that auld.'

'But Mum, you forget things now, it's the drink that's addled your brain, they said.'

'Rubbish.' She huffs, her voice hardens. 'Ye'll come home now, Morven, and get rid of these carers, they just want to keep me a prisoner.'

'Saturday, Mum.'

'Saturday!' She spits that out. I can visualise her in the easy chair in her living room, working hersel up.

'Look Mum. Ye don't need me while I'm at work, so ye can do without me for a couple of days.'

'That's different, I know I can call ye and ye'll come. But now ye're too far away.'

'I'm having a nice time, by the way.'

'Guid for you,' she shouts and hangs up, leaving me staring at the blank screen. I go to press *call* and hesitate. If she's stuck, she can phone the helpline.

I wish I could be strong. Too many memories. Being sent to bed in the afternoons at the weekends whilst Ishbel had her parties, drinking vodka, living beyond her means, a harem of hangers on, women who liked to drink aw night. I'd watch her from my doorway as she sat at her dressing table layering on the heavy make up, then rolling a red lipstick around her thin lips. Dad was a shadow, fading away in his sleep, heart failure. Ishbel the weeping widow, drinking in the living room after the funeral, the stink of abandoned beer bottles and the whisky-soaked carpet. Scarlet nail varnish flashing against the black chiffon blouse. The drinking, the drugs, the parties, the ambulances' flashing lights as they rushed her away, waiting next door wi the neighbour, watching for Grannie to hurry up the path to collect me. Until finally she put her foot down and took me to live wi her.

Now, these tantrums. Everyone against her. The consultant, in his posh voice, counselled, *she's an addict, it's an illness.* Least there's a care plan now. Next stop residential care unless I move in wi her. A cold shiver runs down my spine. Ishbel was stoating at Grannie's funeral and thought some distant cousin was plotting to hurt her. 'Get that bastard oot o here,' she'd screamed, holding on to me for dear life. She grabbed at a pint glass on the table and chucked it across the room at the poor man who was open mouthed wi shock. Some men managed to steer him away whilst I calmed her. Although quietened, she sat steely eyed watching the door.

There'd be nae peace. I've worked hard to build up the business. Many of my customers prefer a female plumber. I wonder if there's anyone like me on Skye. There's potential for renovations here in this very bay. Be an expensive place to rent or buy but wi the cash from the sale of Grannie's flat ... Ex-council, but still worth a fair bit. In a nice spot up the hill wi a guid view of the Elvern as it snakes its way from Loch Lomond to the Clyde. I had a peek at the croft house next door in the twilight last night and it looked possible. Och, a silly dream. It wouldnae likely be for sale or it would've been done up awready.

Ishbel didnae phone back but she'd awready managed to spoil the day. I put off the business till next day and by nine o'clock I'm in my bed.

*

A roll of thunder ower the cottage wakes me wi a sudden start. Sheets of flash lightning brighten the room breaking the dark. I lean ower to switch on the lamp but it isnae working so I spring out of bed and hurriedly check the wall switch. Nae light. Candles? I pick my way up the hauf flight to the living area. Another flash illuminates the room and I make it to the kitchen on the memory of it. I root through the kitchen drawers and find some candles, but what about matches? Under the microwave maybe? Success. Once settled cosy in the armchair I welcome the glowing flames in the grate wi the blanket swathed around my shoulders and tucked under my chin.

Grannie sits on the chair across. It's too noisy for speech so we sit together in flickering candlelight waiting out the storm's temper, its cracking of lightning, its rolls of thunder coming closer in crescendos of violent barks ower the roof, its rain battering the mezzanine window.

The storm recedes wi morning and I go hunting for the electricity box. I flick the switch. The electricity buzzes on. What if there's been damage and the road isnae passable? There's no a shop here in the bay. I check the fridge and the cupboard. Enough provisions for a few days. But what if Ishbel needs me and I cannae get through the mountain?

*

The sea's calmed, thank God, and the wind has more or less died away. The sun's out and everything's a glistening paradise. It's a guid time for Grannie to hit they waves she's spoken about so often. I collect her from the table, place her in the canvas bag, lock up and stride down to the bay in warm sunshine.

I climb ower a load of rocks and shingle until the wet sand starts, and there I have to jump ower rivers of seawater snaking their way to shore. Except for gulls circling above, I'm alone in the bay surrounded by hills on three sides and sea ahead. I taste the freshness of salt sea air on the breeze. A couple of auld croft houses sit on the foothills, and on the cove to the left is a field of grazing sheep. I look around for a suitable spot. Some rocks sit ower there, boulders that look as if they've been dumped by those giants. I spot a pathway between them down to the lapping waves. It's sheltered here and I sit down on a boulder. The rock across has a rough but level shelf to put Grannie on whilst I get ready. I slip off my shoes and socks and roll my chinos up to my thighs. The wind is light, but still blowing wi a slight hiss. I cannae have Grannie come back aw ower me. Well Grannie, I hope this will do you. I'm on your island, on the beach you dreamed about.

I lean ower, lift the solid tube from the bag and pull off the lid. Ash sprays out around my hands and arms. Sorry, Grannie. I should've brought some wellies but bare feet will have to do. Picking my way ower wet sand, I hold tight onto the tube wi both hands. Water trickles through my toes and I jump back in shock.

It's bloody freezing.

I inch my way forward, gasping as the sea rises ower

my ankles to my knees. By the time it's at thigh level I've become acclimatised, it's almost warm. I shake the container so that some ash escapes and I test its trajectory, needing to turn against the wind a bit more. Satisfied, I shake more out. Grannie spills onto the surface of the sea in a plume of smoke. The waves carry her inland but there's enough space for the ashes to be taken wi the water before she reaches the shoreline. I spew the rest into the sea a shake at a time and wish I was religious, but I can only remember some of the *Our Father.* I say that. Then decide to sing a bit of *Hail, Queen of Heaven, the Ocean Star*. The tinkle of children's laughter makes me stop but when I turn full circle there's no one around. It must be the wind playing wi the waves. When the tube is empty, I thump it on the bottom and then soak it in the water to make sure aw of Grannie has gone. I stand still remembering my grannie, and how much I love and need her, whilst the wind wipes away my tears. Then I turn and face the shimmering sun and breathe in the cool salty sea air.

I wade back to the shore and at the water's edge follow my footprints in the wet, dark sand back to the line of boulders. Something's odd. I kneel down. How come? Three sets of prints. Mine going towards the water and mine returning to this point. But there's another line of footprints going one way only, fresh as mine, trailing along the sand where they disappear into the sea.

Awards, Prizes and Previous Publications

The Cailleach of Redgauntlet Close was shortlisted at The Pritchett Prize 2021.

The Boy on the Bridge was shortlisted as Kindred Spirits at Fish Short Story Competition 2016 and longlisted at The Exeter Short Story Prize 2021.

Double Take was shortlisted at Wells Literary Festival 2017, and Frome Festival 2019, longlisted at Parracombe 2021 and published in their anthology.

Tartan Legs was shortlisted at the Hysteria Short Story Competition 2016 and published in their anthology.

Kitten Heels was shortlisted at the Exeter short story prize 2017, and won Ringwood's 2022 short story prize.

Havoc Shore was longlisted at the Fish Short Story competition in 2017, shortlisted at the Short Story Prize 2017, longlisted at Woman and Words 2017, shortlisted for the Bristol Prize in 2018 and published in their anthology.

Fox Fur was longlisted at Bricklane Bookshop Competition July 20 and published in Writers' Forum February 2021 achieving second place.

Ring of Fire was published in Prole 20, August 2016.

Trip Switch was shortlisted at HISSAC competition in 2016, in 2018 it was longlisted at the Fish Short Story Competition, it was longlisted at the Segora Short Story Competition in

2019 and was longlisted at the Exeter Short Story Prize 2019. It was published by Impspired May 2021.

Tiramisu was published by Northwords Now, Spring 2018.

Isa's Pitch was shortlisted at Willesden Herald's short story prize 2017 and published in their anthology.

The Thin Place was longlisted at Frome Short Story Prize 2022 and shortlisted at Evesham Short Story Prize 2022.

Etcetera was shortlisted at Evesham Festival of Words 2017 and published in their anthology.

Heron won The Labello Prize 2014 and was published in their anthology, Gem Street.

It Would Take a Miracle was longlisted at Parracombe Prize 2022 and published in their anthology.

Next Stop won second place at Ringwood's Short Story Competition 2023 and was published on their website.

Blackbird was longlisted at The Leicester Writers' short story competition and published in their 2017 anthology.

Acknowledgements

Thanks to my writing friends who have read and reread countless versions of these stories over the past fourteen years.

Special thanks goes to novelist, poet, and short story writer Patricia M. Osborne for her insight and suggestions.

Also thanks to poet Maggie Mackay, novelist Trish McGrath, poets Corinne Lawrence and Sheena Bradley, and novelist Georgia Davies for their support and encouragement.

I am also thankful for the support of Ringwood Publishing, in particular, Sandy Jamieson, Isobel Freeman, Beatrice Crawford, Olivia Currie, Leah Hart, Luiza Stoenescu and Skye Galloway for her beautiful cover design.

As always, sincere thanks to my family and friends.

I couldn't do it without you.

About the Author

Maureen Cullen is a retired social worker living in Argyll & Bute. After thirty years commitment to social work she turned to writing poetry and short fiction, completing a Master's Degree in Creative Writing from Lancaster University in 2015, achieving a distinction.

Maureen has poetry published in multiple magazines and online webzines, and has a poetry conversation written with Patricia M. Osborne, *Sherry and Sparkly,* published by the Hedgehog Press in 2021.

Maureen has been shortlisted in numerous short story competitions, including the V.S. Pritchett Prize, the Fish Prize, and the Bristol Prize. She also won the Labello Prize for short fiction in 2014, and the Ringwood Short Story competition in 2022.

Maureen's debut novel, *Kitten Heels*, was published in October 2024 by Ringwood Publishing.

Maureen can be contacted through her website at:

www.maureen-cullen.com

X @maureengcullen

Facebook Maureen Cullen Author

Also by this Author

www.ringwoodpublishing.com
mail@ringwoodpublishing.com

Kitten Heels
Maureen Cullen

Kitten Heels is a moving coming-of-age story, set in 1960s working class Clydeside and told from thirteen-year-old Kathleen's perspective. Dealing with issues of poverty, mental health, and the role of women, *Kitten Heels* follows Kathleen as she finds comfort and support in the community of women around her – learning from the way in which these women find ways to grow, nourish and heal each other, despite hardships and institutional obstacles set in their way.
ISBN: 978-1-91701-101-3
£9.99

Printed in Dunstable, United Kingdom